Sight

Jessie Greengrass

JOHN MURRAY

First published in Great Britain in 2018 by John Murray (Publishers)
An Hachette UK Company

First published in paperback in 2019

1

© Jessie Greengrass 2018

The right of Jessie Greengrass to be identified as the Author
of the Work has been asserted by her in accordance with
the Copyright, Designs and Patents Act 1988.

A CIP catalogue record for this title is available from the British Library

ISBN 978-1-473-65239-2
Ebook ISBN 978-1-473-65238-5

Typeset by Hewer Text UK Ltd, Edinburgh
Printed and bound by CPI Group (UK) Ltd, Croydon, CR0 4YY

John Murray policy is to use papers that are natural, renewable and
recyclable products and made from wood grown in sustainable
forests. The logging and manufacturing processes are expected to
conform to the environmental regulations of the country of origin.

John Murray (Publishers)
Carmelite House
50 Victoria Embankment
London EC4Y 0DZ

www.johnmurray.co.uk

Jessie Greengrass

Jessie Greengrass was born in 1982. She studied philosophy in Cambridge and London. *An Account of the Decline of the Great Auk, According to One Who Saw It* won the Edge Hill Short Story Prize and a Somerset Maugham Award, and was shortlisted for the PFD/*Sunday Times* Young Writer of the Year. *Sight*, her first novel, was shortlisted for the 2018 Women's Prize for Fiction.

Praise for *Sight*

'Precise and moving . . . The pages on the mother's decline are a masterclass in wrenching, pitiless truth . . . the potted stories of Röntgen, Freud and Hunter form a fluid, richly associative historic narrative of investigation into the body and the mind' *Daily Telegraph* ****

'Greengrass's fiercely cerebral despatch from one of life's most extraordinary rites of passage impresses linguistically, intellectually and emotionally' *Mail on Sunday*

'The poise, intelligence and serious intent of *Sight* will be lauded, and rightly so' *Sunday Times*

'An outstanding first novel' *TLS*

'There are echoes of W. G. Sebald and Rachel Cusk in this thoughtful, digressive style that swirls together the historical and the personal, but Greengrass's questing intellect and elegant prose are all her own' *Guardian*

'This is a first novel – an original one by a writer who clearly has considerable gifts and a serious, nuanced approach to individual psychology and intellectual history' *Financial Times*

'Jessie Greengrass's first book . . . won plaudits for its incisive, compelling prose. Greengrass brings the same power to her debut novel' *Radio Times*

'Cerebral and tender, Greengrass's voice is smart and original' *Elle*

'Greengrass is undoubtedly that rare thing, a genuinely new and assured voice in prose. Her work is precise, properly moving, quirky and heartfelt' A. L. Kennedy

'Beautiful and devastating and perfectly formed' Daisy Johnson

'One of the finest English novels I've read . . . It is exquisitely well-assembled and every page has a line of pure underline-for-later brilliance' Max Porter

'*Sight* is a beautiful debut, and Greengrass is an important new voice in fiction' Jamie Quatro

For Ada, who made this hard, and made it possible

I

The start of another summer, the weather uncertain but no longer sharply edged, and I am pregnant again. In front of me is all the ordinary and useful disarrangement of my desk and beyond it the rain-smudged window with a view across our garden to where my daughter plays, watched over by Johannes. She has begun to lose, lately, the tumbling immediacy of toddlerhood. I notice it when we walk together, our strides separate, or when we sit face to face across a table – how she is taller now and straighter, and inflects her actions with intent. Once her thoughts broke like weather across her face, but that readable plasticity is gone and she is not so transparent: complexity has brought concealment. The weight of her body when I lift her takes me by surprise, its unfamiliarity a reiteration of the distance between us. She used to clamber over me, her legs around my waist, her arms around my neck, as though I were furniture or an extension of herself, unthought-of or intimately known. Now she stands apart and I must reach for her, on each occasion a little further until it seems her progress towards adulthood is a kind of disappearing and that I know her less and less the more that she becomes herself. This is how things ought to be, her going away while I remain, but still I think that if I could then I might reach across to where she stands, outlined against the violent yellow mass of a forsythia bush, and pull her back to me, to keep her always in my sight so that she might be nothing more than the sum of what I know of her.

On 28 December 1895 at the Salon Indien du Grand Café in Paris the Lumière brothers, Auguste and Louis, presented to the public for the first time a screening of a selection of their cinematographic films. All that afternoon along the Boulevard des Capucines a line of people waited, their breath rising through the freezing air, in expectation of a wonder. Later, sat in rows on slat-backed chairs, they saw it: the flickering black-and-white image of Auguste holding his baby daughter up to a fishbowl, balancing the child on her feet so that she might look down at the water inside, the tumbling elision of the film's frames making manifest inside the winter darkness a months-old summer afternoon – and at the same time, 600 miles away in the Bavarian city of Wurzburg, Wilhelm Conrad Röntgen, chair of physics, ran through the streets to hand over a paper to the president of the university's Physical Medical Society, a first description of the X-ray. For weeks, while the Lumière brothers had prepared their films, Röntgen, alone in his laboratory, its windows draped with heavy cloth to keep the winter's weakened sunlight out, had seen all that had been solid grow towards transparency. Opaque materials – wood, stone, his own flesh – had been reduced for him to shadowed outline, leaving the image of a substrate world spread out across a photographic plate, a catalogue of metal and bone and all that would not rot to set against cinema's preservation of surface—

There was a point, some years ago, when this concatenation of dates preoccupied me. I was trying to decide whether to have a child. For months, all through a wet spring and an early, lightless summer, Johannes and I sat side by side in the evenings on the sofa or in the garden and we talked about it, or we didn't talk about it, but it seemed that we never talked of anything else, all our words mere surtext to my inability to find a way out of the bind in which I had placed myself. I wanted a child fiercely but couldn't imagine myself pregnant, or a mother, seeing only how I was now or how I thought I was: singular, centreless, afraid. I was terrified of the irrevocability of birth and what came after it, how the raising of a child, that unduckable responsibility, might turn each of my actions into weighted accidents, moulding another life without intention into unpropitious shapes, and caught between these two poles – my desire, my fear – I was miserable and made Johannes miserable, too. Minute by minute I would be sure that a decision had been reached but they wouldn't stick: I felt that I was staring at a fissure to be leapt across, and each time, making my feint at its nearer bank, I would run out, and over and over again that year I knelt on the floor in front of Johannes and said

—I don't know what to do, what should I do?

until he could only hold my head in his hands and say

—I love you

because he had exhausted all argument. For him the answer was obvious: we would have a child, and the rest would follow. He didn't fear himself to be inadequate, insufficient to the task of making someone whole, nor see how afterwards, when it was too late, the ground might give beneath our feet to let us fall, the child that we had wanted tumbling through the air between us; and although he was never less than kind he didn't know what to say to me and I began to catch, at times, a hastily suppressed frustration in his voice. During the day, instead of working, I sat at my desk with its view across the garden, empty then, and watched the 42-second-long *La Pêche aux poissons rouges,* the Lumière brothers' film. This is what we cling to at such times: the illusion that in the world there is a solution, if only we can find it, and it seemed to me that into that infant's face, turned towards the curiosity the camera made on a hundred-years-ago Lyon afternoon, a whole child-hood had been distilled, and that if I looked hard enough, absorbing into my own body each detail of the way Auguste's hands held his daughter, of her responding smile as she reached down to pat the surface of the water, then I might understand what it would be like to be either of them. I had no idea how it might function, Johannes and me and a child inside the same house. My own father had slipped out halfway through my childhood, leaving little of himself behind, and my mother had died when I was in my early twenties, her death so desolating that for months afterwards I had been unable to recognise my unhappiness, mistaking the joyless pall I wore for adulthood's final arrival: the understanding, come at last, that the world was nothing but what it appeared to be, a hard surface in a cold light. To fill the space that even grief refused to occupy I had read, at first indiscriminately and widely and then, as I began at last to reconstruct myself, building piecemeal on the foundations of all that had been demolished by my mother's death, on Wilhelm Röntgen and the early history of the X-ray. Now, happening on the coincidence of that single darkening afternoon at the end of the nineteenth century, I began to believe that if I could see how these two events fitted together, the way that simultaneity tied them, then perhaps I might see also through their lens the frame on which my own life had been constructed, its underlying principle, or how it was that I should find myself considering motherhood when it seemed that I had barely altered from unhappy adolescence. Perhaps, too, I might find the guarantee I wanted that in the future I would not fail or fall – but after all there was nothing to it. What I had mistaken for significance was mere concurrence – the burghers of Paris waiting in the street while elsewhere Röntgen ran through an empty university – and so as each long afternoon bled towards its close, as the cat began its plaintive cry for food and as Johannes, working in the room above, began to shift and stir, the floorboards creaking out their sympathetic indication of his winding down towards the evening, I remained as I was, *La Pêche aux poissons rouges* playing over and over on my computer screen, the image of the child and her father, a key which failed to fit a lock.

As a child in the Netherlands, where his family had moved from their native Germany when he had just turned three, Wilhelm Conrad Röntgen showed no particular academic talent. He was marked out, if at all, by little more than a precocious skill with machinery, an imagination articulated from cogs and levers, and a manual dexterity that he would later use to make his own laboratory equipment, believing that it was with this intimacy of construction that insight might be bought. Beyond this he was an ordinary child without particular aptitude for lessons, easily distracted, although possessing a kind of outdoorsy curiosity, an interest in the natural world which in a less solid boy might have been called dreaminess. At the age of seventeen, for refusing to divulge the authorship of a caricature of one of the masters, he was expelled from his technical school in Utrecht without the necessary qualifications for university admittance, becoming instead a student of mechanical engineering at the polytechnic in Zurich, where entrance was by examination rather than qualification; but even after he had moved from there to the university and gained his PhD, coming under the influence and patronage of Professor August Kundt, his lack of a school certificate was a stumbling block, so that it was some years before he could secure an academic position in his own right, moving instead between Würzburg and Strasbourg as Kundt's assistant. By then, though, he had learned the habit of application, an

unfaltering dedication which appeared imagination's opposite, and he tackled these obstacles with the same solid determination with which he approached all aspects of his life – his
marriage, friendships, interests, his work: a steady, unde-
flected, incremental progress towards a goal, each step taken
cautiously, tested and retested so that at the end he could be
sure that what he had made was sound. He retained the metic-
ulousness which as a child he had used to make mechanical
devices, developing an interest in photography and in player
pianos alongside his scientific work, buying a Welte-Mignon
for the drawing room to demonstrate to guests. He also kept
his love of the outdoors, a fondness for snow and winter sports,
spending his autumns in the Engadin mountains and his
springs at Lake Como where he took his wife, Bertha, whose
health was not always good, on excursions in a horse and cart.
By the winter of 1895, six months past his fiftieth birthday, it
seemed that his life had attained a kind of coasting form, the
satisfactory shape of one of his own mechanisms: something
soundly made and set upon a steady course, well-tended,
gently oiled. His position in the university was assured and his
career was an ordinarily distinguished one. He was respected
in his field and his name would be remembered, if not in chapters, then in footnotes and appendices: those places clarity
inhabits, the carefully worked-through detail in which a
subject's virtue lies; and afterwards, after the few short weeks
that he spent working on X-rays before returning to his previous work, after he had written the three papers which were all
that he could find in himself to say on the subject, he seemed

to look back on this smaller renown as something lost, its sudden overturning an act to be regretted.

My mother fell ill shortly after my twenty-first birthday and for a long time, despite the fact that I became responsible, by increments, for her care, I tried to carry on as if nothing was happening, living in the shared flat behind the Elephant and Castle roundabout that I had moved to after leaving university and travelling each morning out to my mother's house, an unprepossessing mid-60s' villa set back behind a driveway deep in the eliding sprawl that seeps for miles beyond the city's boundaries, small towns running into one another under a canopy of trees. This was the house I had lived in all my life but I felt little affection for it, and nor I think did my mother. Our place in it had been built not on choice or fondness but on circumstance, a constant provisionality defined by our wish to leave if only those things which kept us there – work, school, a habit of thought or of routine, the convenient proximity to the city which we valued in principle but rarely took advantage of – could be evaded. Leaving for university three years earlier I had thought myself to have escaped from it at last, the process of growing up an inevitable upward curve, exponential and away – but then my mother became ill and once more I was pulled back. I gave up my attempts to find a job and instead each morning I sat in an empty outbound train to make this journey backwards, watching through the scratched window-pane the full carriages run past in the opposite direction, heavy with their complements of lives. The unfairness of this forced return angered me, but I felt too the impossibility of my anger, the imperviousness of events towards it; and sometimes as I struggled in the morning to force my way to the ticket barrier against the suited tide I felt again the disempowerment of childhood, that awareness of injustice and the futility of its protest. Then, in the evenings, after the hospital appointments and the hours on drips, after the loads of washing done and the twin plates drying in the empty kitchen, after the silent afternoons, the long gap between lunch and tea filled with nothing but the anxious, empty tedium of the ends of lives, I would travel back the other way; or, more often than not, some minor crisis would keep me where I was so that instead of going back to the city I would lie awake in my childhood bedroom listening to the sounds from the garden, the bark of foxes and the hoot of owls where the roundabout's traffic roar should be, and feel that the world was turning elsewhere while I lay, still and confined, rerouted from that easy future which I had assumed would be my right.

By degrees, over the course of the months after her initial collapse, caused by a sudden burst of blood into the soft substance of her brain which, while stemmed, could not be stopped, my mother's illness stripped her of strength and agency. Her muscles were unsprung, her joints unlocked. The medication which she took to keep the worst at bay caused her body to swell, doubling in size to a facsimile of health, her face plump and ruddy. For a while, with a diagnosis made and treatment-regime established, with radiotherapy a fortnightly inconvenience, she had seemed almost well, until that first week during which she had lain pale as paper in a hospital bed became a memory that left us giddy with relief for all it had marked an end to unchecked time. She was tired, perhaps, a little unsteady on her feet, and down one side of her skull, surrounded by a fur of regrowing hair, a scar ran that was the length of my hand and pink and smooth, but although she was not what she had been, neither had she become what I had feared she might, as I had sat amongst the tangle of tubes and monitors, the drips and beeps, and waited for what was left of her to surface from the surgeon's work. Those first weeks, when it still seemed to us that we might pick up our old lives again somehow, had the stolen air of holidays and our sorrow was exultant, a pouring forth of hope and love, because we had not yet felt the truth of it: that there would be no afterwards from which we might look back and count ourselves lucky to have escaped. My mother needed help at first only with domestic chores, with cooking and cleaning and trips to the supermarket, and someone to accompany her on hospital visits, to sit next to her in hot rooms and stare out of windows as bad news was delivered and explained; but as time went on these solid remains of her health began to erode and more and more things became impossible for her. She started to need help moving about the house, climbing steps and manoeuvring herself in and out of chairs and, when her left arm began to weaken, with cutting up her food and washing her face; and so our lives began to fold in around one another, tangling, contracting, her need for me forcing into reverse that inevitable process of separation which was the work of adolescence.

10

We both felt it. As I sponged her head with water to get out the last of the soap from what was left of her hair or as I helped her dress I tried to be kind but for me to be so, for me to try to comfort or to shield her, to be more gentle with her than was necessary for the completion of the immediate task at hand, would have been only to more brutally invert our natural roles, and that itself would have been a kind of violence towards this woman who had always sought to protect me, to soften the impact of the world and keep me safe. We were often silent with one another. It began to seem that the only solution to our physical closeness was an emotional distance – we hid from one another, we shrank apart, until all affection was leached from our touch and only pragmatism, necessity, was left. We allowed practicality to stand in for compassion and my nominal residence elsewhere acted as a boundary line, a point of principled separation, until one morning I arrived at the house to find her curled up on the bathroom floor, asleep, a child's steroidal plumpness at her elbows and her wrists. For weeks, since that part of her brain which governed spatial awareness had begun to fail, she had been unable to dress herself, her knickers having come to represent a geometrical puzzle that she couldn't solve, but now she had lost the ability to navigate from one room to another, becoming confused in doorways, turning herself in odd directions. Although she still recognised the house, although she said that nothing really looked any different to her, and although she still knew that, for example, the kitchen was on the left of the living room and the bathroom at the top of the stairs, when she tried to translate this knowledge into action it confounded her. That mental construct which she had of the house we had lived in for the entirety of my life – the two of us echoing backwards through the sheltering closeness of its rooms, our arguments, our gestures of anger and our reconciliations, our particular celebrations and our daily grinding still present in the marks across the walls and floors, the ghost stains on the carpets, the wonky handle to the study door – this no longer bore any relation to the space through which she moved, the fact of it unparsable even while her memory of it remained clear and detailed. Her body, too, had become strange to her, its shape no longer matching the map she had of it, so that her idea of where she was in space floundered and was unreliable and any movement was a conscious effort of attention, a matter of watching, pushing her body about as though it were mere mechanism while elsewhere, on an empty plane, its mental analogue moved freely through a steady silence. The following day I packed up my room in the Elephant and Castle flat and moved home, stuffing my belongings into a holdall and, when that was full, into plastic carrier bags. I took a taxi to the station and then at last I found myself going in the same direction as everyone else, sat as the evening rush hour began in the corner of a commuter train on top of my unwieldy pile of things. Changing at Clapham Junction one of my bags split, sending a cascade of jumbled paperbacks and underwear slithering down into the gap between the train and the platform to settle on the tracks. I stood in the crowd of homing workers, my dirty jeans and high-tops squalid amongst the multitude of suits and brogues, the remaining bags slouched about my legs, and I watched the trains run again and again across my things—

and if, afterwards, I was unable to see quite how deeply grief ran, if I felt I had no right to my unhappiness, then in part I think it was because I was ashamed that this last journey home was one that I had made, not out of love, nor even from compassion, but only from expediency, because it was necessary and because there was no one else to do it.

In 1890 in the physics department of the University of Pennsylvania, five years before Wilhelm Röntgen made his observations on the effect of a new kind of rays, Arthur Goodspeed placed an unexposed photographic plate beneath a pile of coins on a table next to a Crookes tube, the same piece of equipment that would lead Röntgen to his discovery. Later, when the plate was developed, Goodspeed found on it in place of the image he was expecting a series of small, round shadows, speckled blotches, as though it were the jacket of a book left lying on a window sill for months, its ink bleached by the sun to leave a sharp outline of what had sat on top of it. He kept the plate, because it was a curiosity or a puzzle – and five years later, after he had read Röntgen's paper and seen the pictures which accompanied it, X-rays of weights inside a box or bones inside a hand, Goodspeed repeated the work that he had done before, and found, as he had suspected, that the image was the result of the plate's exposure to X-rays. This picture, reproduced, appears both old and accidental, like liver spots on skin or something spilled, the two circles left by the coins distinct but not entire, their edges collapsing on one side, the blackness of their shadows bleeding into grey, and seeing it I find myself constructing an image of Doctor Arthur Willis Goodspeed, stood in his laboratory with its view across the campus gardens to the Schuylkill river, as he performed with good grace those experiments which would prove that he, unlike Röntgen, had suffered a failure, not of understanding, nor quite of luck, but of something in between – a felicity which is both attention and timing.

Shortly after I first met Johannes we spent an afternoon together at the Victoria and Albert museum. It was a Saturday and I walked to the museum from Marble Arch station, across Hyde Park to the Albert Memorial, skirting the edge of the Serpentine. That week had brought a false spring, a parting of winter's drapes to let through light and air into the early part of March, an unexpectedly warm sun still low enough in the sky that its illumination mimicked that of late summer, September's heavy gold across the bare branches of the trees, the only colour in the flowerbeds from the purple petals of the banked-up Hellebore. By the next weekend drear grey would confine us again to our coats and scarves and we would stay that way for another month or more, but for now there was an impression of unexpected possibility. I was nervous. This outing had been my idea and I was worried about how it might go, that I might have a bad time or that Johannes might, so that one or the other of us would have to stutter our excuses after an hour and leave, the slow disappointed deflation of a hoped-for connection come to nothing. We had, until this point, hardly ever been alone together, meeting only accidentally and in company, through mutual friends, and I was afraid that this alteration in the balance of our relationship would bring with it an awkwardness, or that we would find out that we had, after all, little to say to one another.

Entering through the wide doors that lead in from Cromwell Gardens and walking across the wide atrium of the museum's central lobby, we turned without any particular intent to the right, passing through an arch into the mediaeval galleries, those long corridors with their rood screens and panel paintings, their carvings and assorted armoury, relics of a past which feels at once unimaginable and ordinary, its strangeness quotidian, like a different answer to a familiar question. For a long time we stood in front of an altarpiece, a peculiar, hallucinatory work made in Hamburg towards the end of the twelfth century, two wooden leaves sat either side of a central panel, the whole divided into forty-four smaller squares on which scenes from the Book of Revelation were painted, a meticulous rendering of the coming of the apocalypse. Image by image we were walked through the end of the world: the seven seals opened, the seven trumpets sounded, cracks appeared in the earth. Brimstone fell like black hail and through the narrowing streets of a mediaeval market town, bright rivers of blood carried drowning horses past the burghers leaning out from upper-storey windows: a world at its unmaking. Standing next to Johannes, the footsteps of other visitors cracking through the silence about us, I tried to imagine how it would be to go about one's daily life with this picture hung above it, freshly painted – how it might fade into the background until its horrors would be taken for granted, drifting each day further from notice as they failed to come about. Instead I felt only what enormous coincidence existence consists of that it should have brought that picture here, and us – and how easily, how unwittingly we might break each possible future in favour of another and how, looking back, in place of what had been possible we would see only that thin contingent line, what happened, rising through the vast and empty darkness of what did not.

Afterwards, we wandered through the rest of the museum, the statues and ceramics fading into a grey expanse of time and place, and our conversation was a carefully trivial list of observations until, sitting in the cafe later on, Johannes started to tell me about his family, the unremarkable but intimate details of a variably happy childhood, his absconding English father forgiven, his mother resilient, a tall woman in a tall house with a view across the sea at Harwich, that grey stretch of water somewhere on the other side of which was the place she had been born. These facts, ordinary in themselves, were offered as a gift, a gesture of trust or intimacy made across the table, and searching about for something to show in return I could think only of my own mother, of how her death had seemed like a sudden event slowed down, a single shocking moment that went on for months. All through the summer that came after it, as I slid into grief's silent central eye, falling asleep like a cat in sunny patches, on the corners of settees or curled on rugs, I dreamed that she wasn't dead at all, and had only gone away without telling me; and now she had come back, forcing herself into the shadow-space of her absence – but she no longer fitted. Even in so short a time I had grown and changed – her house was gone and there was no bed for her in the flat I had replaced it with, no extra cup and saucer, no clothes. These dreams were horrible and waking from them I would find my hands clutching at my chest so hard that the nails left crescent indentations in the skin above my breasts. For minutes I would lie, paralysed, until at last the silence of my empty flat began to reassert the truth: that what had happened was immutable and that my grief was earned, awful but particular, a possession whose ownership could not be rescinded.

—My mother died

I said to Johannes, and across the emptiness my words made I extended my hands towards him.

At last, even with me always present, the work of caring for my mother at home became too much. One morning, struggling from her bed to the bathroom, pushing a walking frame in front of her, she stumbled and fell, sitting down heavily on the carpet. She was unhurt but she no longer had the strength to stand back up again and although for a while I tried to right her, tugging her this way and that, bringing various items of furniture to use as props or levers, I was unable to lift her weight. I had to call an ambulance and because she wasn't a priority we sat for hours, side by side on the bedroom floor, waiting for it to arrive. I made us lunch, sandwiches to eat on our knees, the sort of indoor picnic she had made me sometimes as a child on rainy Saturdays, and the fragile cast of this memory brought a kind of complicity between us, a resurgence of the intimacy that we had once possessed, so that for a while it was almost as though we were happy.

When at last the ambulance came the two paramedics between them managed to get her back on her feet. We refused their offer to take us to the hospital and they didn't push, believing, I think, that we were right to do so; but the next day the district nurse came and said that a bed had been made available for my mother at the hospice. I packed a bag for her, a rucksack with spare clothes, her phone and charger, and the book she had been pretending to read for weeks, too proud to tell me that her sight was failing: such a paltry collection of things but after all what else would she need that could be taken from this house. The hospice sent an ambulance of their own to collect us and we tried to give the journey a jaunty air, sucking boiled sweets to keep us from travel sickness in the lurching, windowless interior, and joking with the driver, but the sweets tasted dusty and our jokes fell flat, having the dull clang of cracked bells. Arriving we were shown to a tiny private room and I unpacked my mother's things, plugged in the radio I had brought for us to listen to, went to find the cafe and came back with half-stale pastries. Beyond the rooms for consultations, for art therapy or massage, which made up the ground floor of the building, there was a walled garden, a surprisingly beautiful area of paths and overflowing flowerbeds, jasmine-hung arches and patches of sunny grass, and I said

—We could ask for a wheelchair and I could take you to sit outside. They have a pond—

but she refused, and that was that. A decision had been made, somewhere in the closing corridors of her mind: that she would no longer try to reach beyond herself, nor put aside the business of dying in favour of an experience she had no way of holding on to. She could have been generous. I might have liked to have, later on, this memory of sitting with her watching sunlight fall on water, a last fragment of accord, but she had nothing left to give me now, not even this. Her room became all there was to us, its grubby cream paintwork and its window with a view across the road, its smell of must and disinfectant. For a fortnight she lay on the bed and shrank into herself. Each morning I made this new journey, taking the bus and arriving early to sit beside her bed in the burgundy reclinable armchair that she refused to try and use. I brought her fruit she wouldn't eat, grapes and mangoes, watermelon, and I read to her until she drifted into sleep and then I went and found the nurses or the ambulance drivers drinking tea on their break and told them how important it was that I be able to take my mother home again, my tearful fervour the result of a denial, not of how close my mother was to death, how it shivered about us, a long boundary to be crossed, but of how I wished it would be done because I was exhausted and because there was nothing I could do now but sit and watch, and even that was too much.

I had expected her death to be a radical change, a moment of perceptive clarity after which all would be altered, all rearranged, and so I was unprepared for what came instead: the long descending rallentando of these last few weeks – an extension, by slight degrees, of the gap between my mother's thoughts, her words, her breaths, until at last I was able to stop waiting for the next to come. It was the middle of the night. I had stopped going home some days before and one of the nurses had brought me a blanket so that I might doze, off and on, in the chair by the bed, waking at intervals to see my mother's eyes open or closed, to check the rise and fall of her chest. I thought of nothing and we were quite still; for the first time since her illness had begun I did not wish myself elsewhere. There was nothing to be done or said and nothing to be felt, and I sat and stared out of the window or slept; and on this last night I didn't even sleep but only held my mother's hand, leant forward with my head against her belly as I had lain sometimes in childhood when ill or needing comfort. And then, when I was sure, I pressed the button that hung down on a wire over her bed, and a nurse came, and everything was as it had been except that my mother was gone.

The work that Röntgen began late in 1895 he had been meaning to undertake for the best part of a year but it was only now, as the winter brought about its annual deceleration, returning students, technicians, professors to their homes, that he found the time. It was, to him, a matter of curiosity. He liked to repeat experiments others had already performed, not so much to

check the veracity of their results as because this careful reconstruction, the slow rhythm of test and repeat, brought with it
that particular quality of understanding which is got only by
having seen for oneself: a grasp which is something like illumination, the reframing of proposition to fact so that the truth
of it is felt, immediate. At such times, holidays of sorts when
Röntgen could set aside the strictures of his academic interests
in favour of a kind of happy tinkering, the boundary between
work and hobby blurred, and alone in his laboratory that
winter he began to repeat investigations into cathode rays
which had earlier been performed by two others – by Heinrich
Hertz, who had died on the first day of the previous year at the
age of thirty-six, leaving behind him two small children and a
proof of the existence of electromagnetic rays, and by Philipp
Lenard, whose modifications to the Crookes cathode-ray tube
had included a small, aluminium-covered window, preserving
the pressure inside the tube but allowing the possibility of
escape for the rays whose nature was, through such a process
of deliberate tinkering, slowly being unravelled. Röntgen had
been busy for a week already when on 8 November he noticed
something glowing across the room from which all light had
been excluded, and, walking towards the faint light, he found
discarded on a workbench a sheet of paper which had been
treated with barium platinocyanide, a chemical already recognised as useful because, in the presence of radiation, it would
fluoresce.

Afterwards, Röntgen would become reticent on the subject
of the work he had performed during those weeks. In addition

21

to the paper in which he described his discovery he would give only a single interview, to an American journalist who happened to be passing through Wurzburg during that brief period between the publication of *Über Eine Neue Art von Strahlen* and Röntgen's return to that more ordinary research which constituted, to him, his life's work. This interview was conducted across three languages – German and French, of which the journalist possessed only a partial understanding, and English, which Röntgen spoke as a language of conferences and equipment specifications, a technical dialect sufficient to explain only a sequence of events: the observation of light, the approach towards it – and it seems that the two spoke at cross purposes, their intentions unclear to one another. Röntgen appears to have been baffled by the journalist's interest, his persistent attempts to force Röntgen towards an account, not of the work that he had done, its procedures and its progress, but of the way it had felt to do it. What, the journalist asked, did you think when you saw the faint glow across the laboratory? To which Röntgen answered, 'I didn't think; I investigated—'

but still I can't believe it was so simple, the facts so baldly uninflected by that extra thing that meaning is, the part of truth which is the work of memory and mind, our own felt contribution to the way things are, and so I imagine it like this: the few short steps to bring Röntgen to a halt before the glowing paper as at a reliquary, and then the sudden rush of understanding – an opening up, the world reframed. This is what we cannot help but feel: that surely this was nothing less than gnosis, the penetration of mystery to show the nap of things, a pattern comprehended – and if we could understand these moments and the weeks that followed them when Röntgen, alone, placed object after object in front of his machine and saw them all transformed, then we too might know what it is to have the hidden made manifest: the components of ourselves, the world, the space between.

The effect he had observed could only, Röntgen noted, have been caused by the presence of light but he was certain of his blackout, of the heavy drapes which covered the doors and windows, thickening the darkness. He began to move the piece of paper by increments further and further away from the cathode-ray tube, and then to place what objects were near at hand between the tube and the paper so that he might get an idea both of range and penetration. Within a few minutes it was, he said, clear to him that the source of the glow could only be the tube, that it could not be light escaping because of the shield, and that neither could the phenomenon be the result of cathode rays, whose range was too short and penetration too limited to reach through a sheet of cardboard and across the room – that what he saw was, in short, the activity of a new sort of ray; and over the next seven and a half weeks he would continue his investigations, testing the limits of what, in honour of its unknown quality, he dubbed the X-ray.

Later there would be a persistent discomfort even amongst Röntgen's supporters about the ease of his discovery, the way it came from nowhere like an unexpected present, and perhaps it is true to say that this knowledge was something waiting to be found, hardly even buried. He was not even the first – as well as Arthur Goodspeed there was Philipp Lenard who, while pursuing those investigations earlier that year which Röntgen was repeating, had observed the same fluorescence but had failed to recognise the significance of it, this softly glowing indicator of the presence of something new. Unlike Goodspeed, who would take with such grace his understanding of what he had almost seen, Lenard held this failure against Röntgen for the rest of his life. His own oversight had been, he considered, a matter of ill luck, his failure to explore or to document what he had observed a function not of decision but of circumstance; and so how could Röntgen's success have been anything but the opposite. Had it not been him it would have been someone else that winter, or early the next spring, any of those who that year set up their electrodes and their tubes and ran their currents through to see what they might find, and if that was the case then perhaps Rontgen's experience was little more than treasure trove; but we cannot deal so easily in counterfactuals. To say that something other might have been is not to diminish the value of what was, the marvel of it or its solidity, besides which it is not the fact of Wilhelm Röntgen's discovery which fascinates but rather it is those days and nights through which he worked alone, bringing to this mystery's unravelling all of his slow, systematic persistence until he possessed not just the sight of something but that extra thing that knowledge, understanding, is – not the mere serendipity of discovery but the moment of its tipping into insight which draws our lonely curiosity. We are unsatisfied.

24

Revelation is by definition isolate, it can neither be communicated nor transferred, and trying to comprehend it we feel only the chill of our exclusion.

For months my purpose had been imposed by circumstance, the structures of my life externally defined so that I had been like a creature inside an exoskeleton, soft and pulpy, held to shape by a rigidity which was not my own, and I had resented it. I had felt that control of my life had been taken from me to be housed elsewhere, amongst the articles of chance, the lottery tickets and the slot machines, the hopes for better weather – but waking on the morning after my mother's death to a house that felt as empty as the body in the half-lit hospice room, having for the first time in months slept as long as I had wanted and feeling sickened that my initial experience of this redrawn world was relief at being rested, I lay in bed waiting for a call to drag me from it, the pressing urgency of someone else's need, and when none came I was stranded, and could only lie and wait as around me the shadows moved slowly across the walls of my outgrown room. I had felt the first shock of this abrupt redundancy the previous night. In answer to my pressing of the bell a nurse had come and as she began to move quietly about my mother's bed, checking and re-checking, ordering, I stood awkwardly by and watched her, my expulsion from a world that I had occupied for months abrupt, my role as carer curtailed by the absence of anyone to be cared for. After a few minutes I began to gather up the belongings that over the past few weeks had been spread about the room, a scarf and hat, the book I had been reading, my house keys left on the table by the door, and it was as though I were packing up a hotel room after a night's residency, erasing all traces of myself to return it to the anonymous state in which I had found it, ready for its next inhabitant.

Eventually, the private ritual of her immediate tasks completed, the nurse turned her attention towards me

—This way, my love,

and I could have cried at the endearment, its tacit acknowledgement that I was not quite an adult yet and all this was more than I could find my place within; but I didn't, my dry eyes a first indicator of the silence which would fill my skin to bursting for the best part of a year. She led me to another room, a softly lighted space with seascapes on its walls and, on the small tables that sat at intervals between the furniture, glossy plants whose leaves concealed a multitude of tissue boxes. I suppose it must have been used for this purpose only, that small and quiet room: as a place for the recently bereaved to sit, to contain them while the necessary procedures were put in place, and everything about it was designed to fade into the background, a physical iteration of the noise the nurses' shoes made on the building's carpets – a gentle, hardly audible shush-shush which was somehow less noticeable than nothing would have been. I waited. I didn't want to return to the room my mother's body was in, had nothing more to say nor any need to add to the store of memories I had, the majority of them shadowed already into near-invisibility by the details of her dying face, her chilly hands, but when the nurse returned

26

to take me back to the room that neither my mother nor I could occupy any longer I lacked the energy to refuse and instead followed her to where my mother's body lay. The lights had been dimmed now, and someone, out of a kindness that was sharp as pity, had taken one of the yellow stargazer lilies from a vase by the bed and folded my mother's hands around it, evening out at the same time the position of her body, smoothing the sheets so that whereas before, rumpled and lined, she might have looked asleep, now she was incontrovertibly dead. It was not a comfort to me to see her this way, as though she had been dressed for the occasion. It didn't make any more acceptable those other things, all the accumulated worry of the days and nights before, the unbreeched sadness, the things unsaid, the white foam which had filled and refilled her mouth during the last evening, rising upwards from her failing lungs, or the absenting, her slow withdrawal from me which was so much like being left behind – but still it was something: the transformation of this specific, immediate instance of dying into a standard form. The folded hands, the flower, the sheet were all conventions, recognisable from a thousand paintings, pictures, pointing my path as buoys do at sea away from dangerous currents and into a mapped channel, custom stepping in where my own map had failed. It was a ritualisation, and with it came an offer of entrenchment into a prescribed routine which, accepted, would carry me forwards, allowing me a tiny insulating distance from the cold reality of things, and it was this which saved me the next morning, too, the need to start passing on the news forcing me

27

out of bed, and it kept me going through the days that followed, the business of mourning setting me a course to follow so that my thoughts might rise away from me to nothing – the funeral to be arranged, condolence cards to read and answer, visitors to be fielded or received until everything that needed to be done had happened and, elsewhere, normality had commenced its slow return. Beyond the walls of my mother's house, things again began to move as they had before, I could hear them hum, but there was no place for me – I had no past life, no extant position to step back into; the world was a sum to which I was remainder – and I was adrift, a near-ghost, insubstantial. Those tasks which had previously filled every hour of the day – the shopping and the cooking, the cleaning, the washing up – were now discharged in minutes, with the time left over aching out around me. Even the house disowned me. My mother's belongings lay where she had left them, her shoes in the lobby, her scarf knotted round the banister, and in a drawer spare glasses, unused stamps, these objects enacting a mourning within which I was not made welcome. I spent an afternoon trying without success to pay an electricity bill but my mother's name was still on the account and no one at the electricity company would talk to me. Finding myself cold, the wind worrying at the doors and stripping the leaves from the trees, I tried to bleed the radiators but only ended up with foul-smelling water on the bedroom floors. I didn't know how to replace the salt in the dishwasher or reset the boiler. A bulb blew in the porch light but the shade needed a key to open it which I couldn't find and so darkness pooled, accusatory, around the front door. All these things reproached me, my tiny failures accumulating in drifts about the corners of the rooms – all this arcana of ownership which my mother hadn't thought to tell me and which it hadn't ever seemed the right time to ask about, and now was lost, so that I could never be more than interloper here, my feet treading unwelcome grooves across the carpets—

This is where grief is found, in these suddenly unfilled cracks, these responsibilities – minute, habitual – which have lain elsewhere for years and which, having failed amongst grief's greater broil to be reapportioned, are overlooked in favour of the more dramatic, until even the ordinary starts to crumble. If I thought, all through those freezing months I spent alone in a house whose owner had abandoned us, that I did not grieve, then it was because I had been expecting something else – something both larger and lesser, a monument or a mountain, simple, scaleable, and not this seeping in of space to undermine the smooth continuance of things. I had thought that loss would be dramatic, that it would be a kind of exercise, when instead it was the emptiness of everything going on as before and nothing working as it ought.

Having nowhere else to go all winter I stayed there, in my mother's house that I had never wanted to return to, narrowing myself down until I lived between my bedroom and the kitchen while the rest of it lay empty about me, the disorderly, reproachful quiet of its closed rooms undisturbed, until at last, as the crocuses began to flower in the muddy garden borders, the house was sold. Then I was faced with the problem of what to do with all my mother's things. I felt that I was expected, somehow, to keep them, to make myself curator, but the thought of storing this detritus of an ended lifetime, of dragging it behind me like a deadened limb, turning myself into little more than a conduit for memory, was horrifying; and so in the end I gave away what I could to anyone who wanted it and hired a skip for the weekend to deal with the rest. Across the augmented stillness of an Easter weekend its yellow maw sat in the driveway and I fed things into it, books and photographs, letters, odds and ends of furniture and boxes of knick-knacks, jewellery, clothes – from Friday to Monday I carried things out to it in armfuls through a steady, penetrating rain whose ruinous action spared me from need for second thoughts, and instead of sadness I felt a kind of soaring joy, as though each armload lightened me, and at times I felt that I could hardly contain it but that it must bubble out as laughter to mix with the sound of the rain – except that for the four nights during which the skip sat outside the house, before a lorry came in the early hours of Tuesday morning to drive it away, I found myself unable in the evenings to draw the curtains on it and so I sat, darkness flowing inwards, keeping a kind of vigil, until at last the house was empty and so was I.

Over dinner in a restaurant sometime during that year when I was trying to find the courage to have a child Johannes said, searching for a subject that would have the magnitude to eclipse, however partially, the one we wished to avoid

—You never talk about your mother,

and I was surprised, because it seemed to me that her death had been the defining event in my life and that I talked about it endlessly, a muttered thrum beneath all other conversation. Trying to describe her, though – to lay out on the sanded wooden tabletop between the sea bream and the steak those things which had made her singular – I found myself able to name only her physical characteristics, the least order of things, and even these were cut not directly from memory but from photographs – the black-and-white strip of passport pictures which had fluttered out one day from between the pages of a copy of Elizabeth Bishop's letters, my mother's unsmiling expression set above the square neck of a cotton frock, or the picture of her standing on a beach, bent over to examine something half-buried in the sand, her bobbed hair tucked back behind her ears. These static faces were as far from hers as a shape is from its mathematical description – they conveyed nothing of her but were all that remained to me to describe. It was not that I had forgotten – I could feel quite clearly how it had been, as a child, to hold her hand, what surety of comfort it had brought me and how, the first time I had been sent to my grandmother's alone in the summer holidays, I had cried every morning, waking to a house which reverberated with her absence, and spent the days in listless moping until at last she came to fetch me; and I could remember how it was to listen to a telephone ringing in the certainty that she would answer it, and the particular tilt her head made as she read – but these things were obdurate of explanation. My memory of her, what remained, was like a memory of distance or the cold, intangible, unsymbolic, not sight nor sound, not touch, not taste, and my attempts at a description of it floundered like the description of music does in words, conveying nothing of its sound or substance. Instead, sat opposite Johannes in the restaurant, searching for something to say, it was the image of the skip that came to mind – the shadow that it made in the light cast out by the living room windows, the rain slanting down towards it; and I thought, although I didn't say it, that the truth was that my mother's death, coming as it did so exactly at that turning spot between adolescence and adulthood, had fractured my life, breaking it into two parts, the second one a product not only of the first but of the first plus its curtailing, built to fill the space its end had made – and so it was hard to think about my mother, to speak about her, without acknowledging that it was impossible to wish she hadn't died, because without her death I would have been undone.

After we had finished eating Johannes and I walked for a while along the Embankment, past Blackfriars Bridge towards St Paul's, the cathedral's floodlit bulk against the glass and metal towers of the city a reassurance like the promise of continuity, the persistence of things. It was a relief to be walking like this, side by side, my hand burrowed into the crook of Johannes' arm, feeling the familiar scratch of his coat's tweed against my skin. Like this, freed by the rhythm of our steps from the need to fill silence with speech, I felt the scurrying rat-wheel of my thoughts begin to still, and I could almost believe that I had come to a decision; except that as soon as we stopped walking I knew that the whole thing would start up again. We had taken to spending evenings out like this, in restaurants or in bars, at concerts or talks in which we had only the most cursory interest, as though to make a pass at happiness or because it gave us something else to talk about, the whole city and all the people in it a distraction from ourselves and from the space that spread between us, a membrane's thickness but so wide – and from all the other choices which we couldn't make until this one was settled, from every part of our lives which was made provisional by my indecision, and from the way I rattled to the touch. Often, afterwards, we would walk home instead of taking the Tube, spinning the evening out, deferring the moment when we would arrive at our house and be confronted by all that we had left inside. Walking bought us the right to easy silence and I found that all evening I would look forward to it, the brief and quiet concord which came with the recollection of how things had been when the question of children was still in the future, its distance lending me the certainty of hypothesis: that Johannes and I would have a child, but not yet. As we neared the steps which led upwards to the wide flank of London Bridge I turned my head to look at him, this man I loved or thought I loved, not knowing always what it meant to do so beyond the sharing of bills and preferences, the ordinary ways our lives grew to synchronise and intertwine. We climbed up towards the road and I watched the way the shadows fell across his cheeks, the way his forehead creased, the hooding of his eyes by heavy eyelids, these features as familiar to me as my own skin but his mind elsewhere, a place I could not gain admittance to, and I wondered what I would remember of Johannes, if he were no longer there – which of his particulars I could list that would convey the least measure of how it felt to walk with him like this, the easy placidity of his company, the salve it was and the certainty spreading out beneath our feet like the solid city pavement that what engulfed us now was temporary, that it would be resolved and that we would survive its aftermath – and for a moment, despite the fold of his coat caught between my finger and thumb, he seemed impossibly distant from me, not only unreachable but unfamiliar, a singular instance of the whole he made, both precious and strange, his likeness uncatchable by anything other than himself; and I moved closer to him, holding more tightly to his arm, as though in doing so I might reach across the gulf which kept us separate, that unmeasurable gap between subject and object, and catch hold of all he was and I was not, and keep it safe.

After my mother's house was sold I moved to a flat in the East End of London, somewhere in Hackney's most unlovely parts, close to the canal. The flat was on the first floor of a solid concrete block, a place of extraordinary ugliness, and I think that this was partly why I chose it – because I didn't want to feel that I had benefitted from my mother's death, that her loss had been instrumental in purchasing even the small happiness that a pleasant place to live would have constituted. This flat's rooms were boxy, its ceilings low, and both kitchen and bathroom were floored with the same peeling, nicotine-yellow lino. Through the thin walls my neighbours' lives filtered – their conversations and their television programmes, their cooking smells. Damp rose. The furniture, an ill-assorted collection of chairs and tables, refused to cohere into anything approaching comfort, and as weeks passed I continued to feel that I was waiting for something to happen, a final marker of my residence which would make me feel welcome here, banishing the persistent impression that, even when I was in it, the flat remained unoccupied. My days drifted. It seemed that I existed in a kind of hinterland, lost between an end and a beginning, my life ruptured in a way I couldn't resolve. Those friends whom I had seen often before my mother's illness I felt unable to contact, the necessary explanations being too weighty to bear thinking of. I was lonely but I couldn't see that I was, except at particular times, waking from dreams of company or hearing laughter come through the walls from the flat next door, when I felt it acutely, a sudden awareness of constriction. It was as though I had been ousted from myself, my flat and featureless mind an unfamiliar landscape to which I had only partial access. I couldn't concentrate. I had no appetite, for food or for anything else, and I had almost no energy. No matter how much I slept I still felt the need for more, my limbs heavy and my eyelids sluggish – the sort of all-consuming, intractable tiredness which I have since felt only in the early months of pregnancy. I had nothing to do, no job, no interests particularly, but I felt that to succumb to inactivity would be to welcome that spectre of my own emergent failure, ill-defined but insistent, which haunted the space around me, so each morning at half past nine when the Tube fare tipped over to off-peak I took the train into central London and walked down the Euston Road to the library at the Wellcome Collection. There I would leave my bag in the cloakroom and, scanning my reader's card at the library's turnstile, make my way to a small room at the back where there was a window that could be opened a few inches to let in the heavy, traffic-sodden summer breeze, and then for a while I pottered about, laying my belongings on one of the desks, my handful of unlidded pens set square beside the dog-eared notebook I always carried, my jumper folded neatly down, my phone silenced and sat on top of it. That done I would wander through the library in search of something to read, running my hands along the shelves until I found a subject that caught my attention. I read not with any particular object in mind, nor really with the intention of retaining any information about the subjects that I chose, but rather because the act of reading was a habit, and because it was soothing and, perhaps, from a life-time's inculcated faith in the explanatory power of books, the half-held belief that somewhere in those hectares upon hectares of printed pages I might find that fact which would make sense of my growing unhappiness, allowing me to peel back the obscurant layers of myself and lay bare at last the solid structure underneath.

All morning in the library I would sit at my desk, flicking through contents pages and indexes, appendices, photo captions, chapter headings, following this lead or that a little way until I became distracted or until it was time for lunch, a slice of quiche or tart and a salad in the library cafe, and then often in the afternoons I would give up even that pretence of activity, setting a book to lie open in front of me, the pages rustling softly in the breeze from the open window, and allow myself to drift through the brackish backwaters of the afternoon, the roar of traffic from the road outside a lulling constancy. I stayed each day until the library was almost closed, until the assistant librarians came round with their trolleys to pick up that day's cast-off texts and until the sound of a hoover started up in a distant corridor; and then at the last possible moment, dragging my feet, I would dawdle back out into the street – and although at the time the sound of pages turning seemed to grind against me until I worried that I might be worn away by it to nothing, now I recall that long summer as though it had been spent within the papery confines of a cocoon. I had been reduced to nothing, and now I sought amongst so many books a way to understand myself by analogy, a pattern recognised in other lives which might be drawn across my own to give it shape and, given shape, to give it impetus, direction. The things which I learned without noticing all through that year recur to me still, those images from medical textbooks, the bodies dissected or described, the case notes and the cabinets and all the many ways there are to see inside ourselves, and still I feel that, correctly understood, they might constitute a key—

Each evening when the library shut I walked home, an hour's steady, thoughtless progress through the evening streets with their clots of drinkers outside pubs, their newspaper sellers and fruit stalls, skirting north through the decaying Georgian streets above King's Cross towards the gentility of Islington's garden squares and then down onto the towpath to walk along the canal into Hackney. On one side of me, small brown fish darted between drowned carrier bags and bicycle wheels lay submerged in three feet and six inches of slow water, and on the other, beyond a tangle of vegetation, clumps of catmint mixed with goosegrass, lavender with dandelions, a peculiar combination of intention and neglect, rose the solid, damp Victorian brick wall that sheltered the canal, in its sunken bed, from the city beyond. It was cooler down there, with the water and the shade, than it was above, where the city had spent all day absorbing heat and now let it go, the pavements shimmering slightly in the dusk. In that narrow passageway left over from an older iteration of the familiar city I felt that I could breathe again, and as Haggerston gave onto London Fields and the sharp striations of gentility and grime above the towpath began to meld into a kind of uniform grubbiness, when darkness was beginning to spread through the evening air like ink, I felt at last a brief alleviation of my disconnection from myself and for a quarter of an hour, before I reached the steps which led back up to road level and the entrance to my building, everything else fell away, and for that short stretch I felt only what I was: young, adrift, bereft.

At Johannes' suggestion I spent a weekend by myself, staying in a tiny stone-walled cottage in a valley near Hay-on-Wye. It might, he said, help me to think. Perhaps without him there I might feel less pressure to articulate what was on my mind and might instead be able to concentrate, and so might find myself able at last to come to a decision. He kissed my cheek and said

—Whatever you decide will be all right,

and I tried not to append my own clauses: that he wished only that I might decide, one way or the other, because he had begun to find my indecision intolerable; but Johannes was not so unkind. It was only I who felt the pressure – the pronged implement which caught me was wholly of my own devising. Sometimes, when I saw a woman in a cafe pick up a baby from a pram, I felt a weight in my own arms, a heaviness where nothing was, and the force of my longing for a child was such that I had to turn away but still I could only feel how impossible it was that I should ever manage such uncomplicated love. I took the train to Hereford and then the bus to Hay and from there I walked, my rucksack heavy with provisions, the few miles further into Wales to where the cottage was, its windows facing down the long corrugation of the valley. There was a tiny garden with a bench, a handkerchief of lawn, an apple tree, a single bedroom with a sloping ceiling and an iron bedstead. Arriving, putting cheese on toast under the grill and pouring myself a glass of wine, I thought that in such a place, so simplified, I couldn't fail to find a way to think, but thinking without context is a near impossible activity. I tried to focus my mind, sitting down at the kitchen table half-drunk to write a list of pros and cons, but the effort was ludicrous and I only felt ashamed; instead I drank more and read my way along the shelf of detective novels that sat beside the bed. I missed

Johannes desperately. While at home I often felt that my love for him was intangible, out of reach, an emergent quality that I struggled to locate amongst the objects which filled our lives, the dirty dishes and the small change for the window cleaner, the arrangements for visits to his mother's house, the constant flow of words on minute variations of domestic trivia; but without him I could feel nothing else, love filling the space his absence made, and I wished I could go home, leave the green serenity that I had longed for and return to our dishevelled, smog-blackened house – wished, even, that I could return to the complicated discontent the last six months had been, if only it would mean his hands, his voice; but he had sent me here and how could I return without reaching a conclusion – and anyway I would walk back through the door and all this certainty of love would fade behind the unwashed windows and the unbought milk to the usual chafing familiarity with one another. I sat the week out, unhappy, and went home to tell him with defiance that I wouldn't have a child; but two days later I cried and said that after all I might, because still I could feel nothing but how much I wanted to.

As August failed into September the year after my mother died I began to suffer from headaches, near-migraines which were unlike anything I have experienced either before or since. For months I had drifted further and further away from myself. The faces of strangers caught sight of in the street, or on the opposite escalator as each morning I descended into the station to make my journey to the library, appeared familiar, rising suddenly out of the jumble like friends I had forgotten, their likenesses caught and lost again. The line between recognisable and unrecognisable blurred and the world appeared fragile, glassy and flat, so that I felt that it might shatter if I touched it, falling to my feet in shards to reveal whatever solidity was hidden underneath. Sounds – the grind of traffic, the voice of a man calling from a doorway, a radio spilling outwards from a windowsill – were both muted and precise, as if they were passing through some medium more viscous than air, but the pain of my headaches was something different again. I was incapacitated by it for days at a time, prostrate on my bed with the blinds pulled down and the curtains drawn across them, pain turning the passing of days and nights into the ticks of an excruciating clock, indefatigable and cruel. I felt as though there was something swelling inside my skull, an abscess filling slowly with whatever stuff unhappiness is made of, its edges pressing against the bone like mud against stone, extruding into my sinuses, my eye-sockets, squeezing through my tear ducts and down my throat. Sometimes, at night, when exhaustion would briefly overcome pain and I would pass into a fitful doze at last, then I would dream that my mouth was filled with something like wet sand, a claggy, white substance which regenerated as fast as I could spit it out or excavate it with my fingers from the space between my gum and cheek; and waking I would have the taste of it still, the lingering memory of something like rotten milk catching in my throat.

Afterwards, as the pain receded, I would feel weak and new, a beach scoured clean and still unmarked, and I would lie on sheets stiffened with sweat and watch the dust motes fall slowly through the light which slanted down between a gap in the curtains, feeling the tiny chill of each indrawn breath, and I would wait until I had the strength to totter to the kitchen and pour a glass of water from the tap, lifting it with both hands to my mouth to feel it run into me, and it would be as though I had been reduced to almost nothing, my skin a fragile membrane parting light and liquid. Beforehand, though, in the days leading up to an attack, I would feel glorified. For twenty-four hours I seemed to glow, my body's radiance reflected back to me from every surface of the world to be reabsorbed and retransmitted, a refiner's fire which sharpened as it grew, and I was ecstatic. I teetered on the brink of visions. Revelation pended, the veil between myself and understanding was in a constant state of almost-rending, and I thought I could see shadows through it, the outlines of an as-yet uncomprehended truth, until all at once the mania crested and what came out of it, in place of elucidation, was agony, my head pinned in a vice, my body hanging limp below it, a disarticulated sack of bones and blood around which my limbs curled, stiff and liable to snap. Still, though, for almost two months I did nothing. After each attack the memory of pain was erased, but I could recall clearly how it had felt to be so enraptured and how the aftermath had been, that hollow peace that was so much like resurrection, and I wondered if it might be worth it. At other times, as the pain began and brought with it the certainty that nothing could be recompense for this, I was afraid, sure now that that there was something really wrong with me and not wanting to know what it was, so that it wasn't until the period of these cycles had shortened to leave barely space between them to restock the fridge and wash and dry the bed sheets in preparation for the next headache, that I finally made an appointment to see a doctor.

Bertha Röntgen was used to lost hours, to her husband's absorption in his work which kept him away from home or returned him only in part, his mind elsewhere across the dinner table or as they sat with the fire between them in the drawing room where the piano was; still, though, even she began to worry as, by mid-November 1895, he had taken to sleeping in his laboratory, to taking his meals there, returning to the house only to wash and change his clothes while Bertha watched him, trying hard to keep both concern and curiosity in check. Later, Röntgen would try to diminish what these weeks had been. He would seem to feel keenly Philipp Lenard's attempts to discredit him, the rumours muttered from the sides of mouths that his achievement had been nothing but an accumulation of serendipity. Even the speed with which his friends came to support him was felt as accusation – the suggestion left open by their quick defence that there were charges to be answered. 'It is almost,' he would write some years later, 'as though I had to apologise for discovering the rays' – and by late spring he would have done all the work on X-rays that he would ever undertake, publishing three papers and giving a single lecture. Such was his determination to avoid the subject that when, in 1901, he was awarded the inaugural Nobel Prize for Physics he declined to speak; but, whatever he might have come to feel afterwards, on the subject of those few weeks his own words betray him. The account of his work that he gives in *Über Eine Neue Art von Strahlen*, written hastily through the scrag-end of December to meet the Physical Medical Society's deadline, is a description cried aloud while still in flight, an account of actions performed while hours slipped past like river water, while the world remade itself in front of him, its solid surfaces dissolved to offer up their innards to his gaze; and the speed with which he wrote it, his figure running through the frozen Würzburg streets, is an indicator of his awareness of how fragile was his claim to priority and how much, reflexively perhaps but certainly, he wanted it. While Bertha sat in an empty house and tried to keep her worries to herself, Röntgen in his laboratory reached for whatever was to hand, to hold it up in front of his machine. 'I have,' he wrote, 'observed and photographed many . . . shadow pictures. Thus, I have the outline of a door covered with lead paint; the image was produced by placing the discharge tube on one side of the door, and the sensitive plate on the other. I have also a shadow of the bones of the hand; of a wire upon a bobbin; of a set of weights in a box; of a compass card and needle completely enclosed in a metal case; of a piece of metal where the X-rays show the want of homogeneity . . .' For seven weeks and three days Röntgen existed in a private world transformed for him and him alone, and perhaps this too was a part of his later bitterness: that despite this experience of revelation, the conferral on him of a scientific grace, afterward nothing was different at all, and although he had seen through metal and seen through flesh to what was hidden, and although he had known, or thought that he had known, its nature, what had been left afterwards was only so much quibbling at the bill.

At last, on 22 December 1895, Röntgen broke his run of solitude. Returning home he found Bertha, who for weeks had been his placeholder, moving through the routine business of their lives to keep the edges of it taut on his behalf, and he asked her to come with him. Without questioning she put on her coat and gloves, and together they walked through the winter streets and then through the university, their footsteps echoing in its empty corridors, until at last they reached the door of his laboratory, and Röntgen opened it and pushed her through. For a few minutes, while Bertha stood, uncomfortable in this space which belonged to a version of her husband she knew only by reputation, he moved about, making sure of his equipment; and then without flourish he turned out the light and laid his wife's hand on a photographic plate. Bertha stayed still, doing as he asked of her, while he prepped the Crookes tube and shot the current across it, her hand an object sat between them in the darkness. It took ten minutes for Röntgen to develop the picture, the only sounds his footsteps and the ticking of the regulator clock which hung on the wall above them, and then it was done and, the lights on again, they looked at it, this picture which has become Bertha's enduring image: her skeletal hand, open, fingers curved above the convex length of her palm. Across the lower phalange of her fourth finger Bertha's wedding ring is an uncompromising mark, its blackness against the shadow of her bones a marker of the metal's immutability. Röntgen, who for weeks had been alone in his newly understood world, had sought with this image Bertha's admittance to it, the making of the picture a gesture of both initiation and affection: the tenderness of her bones made visible to them both, confirmation of the life which had formed such extraordinary structures; but these things are a matter of interpretation. To Bertha, whose hands were solid, whose body unitary, who had not doubted those things that constituted her – her skin, her thoughts; the single object that was flesh housing mind – nor sought to understand them, it had the chilly, soily smell of tombs.

—It is,

she said

—like seeing my own death—

and she turned away, and refused to look again.

After I returned from Hay, Johannes and I clung to one another. Something had changed between us: Johannes no longer reassured me that things would be all right and I no longer tried to talk about my fears because to do so seemed to wound him and I wanted above all that he should not look so sad. There was a breaking distance in the way we were so careful with one another. Although we were in contact with one another always, a hand on a shoulder, a leg slung across a knee, our fingers reaching out to twine about the other's, it was not for comfort but rather because it felt that to let go would be to risk a loss that would be absolute. At night we lay awake, our arms around one another, and although in the silence we pressed ourselves together, trying to reach one another, between our naked bellies there was a barrier that we couldn't break and we remained apart. Once from nowhere Johannes cried

—I can't bear it,

but I could offer no comfort, not even that which comes from conjoint suffering.

In the end it was nothing at all which brought resolution. We went away, together this time, walking for ten days in Cornwall along the coast path from Falmouth round the Lizard to Land's End as though in this steady progress westward we might outdistance ourselves. We walked until my mouth filled with the taste of salt and iron, scrambling from sea to cliff-crest and back again with the turn of each cove, hours of arduous labour lost in the traversal of a few straight miles. Once, pausing for breath, looking out from the edge of the cliff at the sea five hundred feet below, we saw a peregrine falcon hovering barely an arm-span away from us and almost on a level, watchful and still, its spotted grey wings barely moving in the updraft, and I felt myself touched by something – privilege perhaps, or luck – that came, after so many months, like a sight of the first green growth through winter earth. We carried a tent, split between our two packs. At the end of each day's walking my skin was covered in a rime of salt, half sweat and half evaporated surf, so that rubbing my fingers on my face it came away in grubby curls, and after dinner in one pub or another we crawled into our tent before dark and in the gentle, subaquatic murk the canvas made of the evening sun, we slept. We barely spoke to one another. At first it was because we had nothing to say that had not been said already but by the middle of the week I felt that it was because we had been emptied out, poured into the rough path, our thoughts nothing more than surface, as routine and repetitive as the passage of the summer breakers up the beaches. In our matched strides we had found a mute accord which had been lacking for months, our only current concerns the cresting of each rise and the need to reach a campsite in time to pitch a tent before the pubs stopped serving dinner. The weather for most of the week was uniformly clear and hot and in the middle of each day we scrambled down off the path to the sea and ate our packed lunches side by side, facing out across the North Atlantic, bread and cheese and packets of crisps after which I swam, the water so clear that I could see shoals of tiny blue fish in it; but on the last day it rained, a thick and heavy summer storm, the clouds descended down low so that air and water merged into a heavy, directionless grey spume and when we reached Land's End at last we couldn't even see as far as the edge of the point. We waited in line with all the other thwarted sightseers to have our picture taken by the signpost to John O'Groats and felt a sense of disjunction, after the solitary days, to be surrounded by such crowds of people, all of them looking askance at our dirty faces and the soaking, mud-splattered clothes we'd been wearing all week. Sitting on the bus back to Penzance we said how funny it was to have been striving so hard to reach a place so completely lacking in any kind of peace or beauty, so forbidding of contemplation, as though we had undertaken a pilgrimage to a supermarket, and we laughed. At the station we booked ourselves onto that night's sleeper and spent the balance of the afternoon and early evening drinking in the station bar, our wet things steaming on a radiator, and I realised, standing on the chipped tiles of the pub toilet looking in the mirror at my half-burned face, that at some point in the week I had outdistanced my anxiety. After all, my decision had been made months ago. I knew that I wanted a child and it was only the point of crossing from the abstract to the particular which was at issue, that gap I saw between myself and the people who were mothers already, my fear of being found wanting, but I was not alone – there was Johannes, strong where I was not, and after all we were only people and a part of us was made for this, I wouldn't fail any further than others did; but most of all I had exhausted myself with indecision and was too tired for any more of it. I wanted to think about something else. I wanted the whole thing to be over and done, and the only way for that to happen was for me to do that thing which I had wanted from the start.

Reading Röntgen's paper for the first time one sunny afternoon at my desk in the library I had been able to follow the thread of it with comparative ease; and surely this was the last time that such a feat was possible: the framing of a radical scientific discovery in ordinary language, the ability to impart understanding without first having to construct a language in which to do so. Röntgen's description of his work comes like the unravelling of a magician's illusion which, explained, quickens rather than diminishing, the understanding of its working conferring the illusion of complicity – the impression that we, too, might be so deft, so sure; and within weeks of the paper's publication interest in it, both academic and popular, had exploded. During 1896, forty-nine books and 1,044 scientific papers were published on the subject of X-rays, as well as newspaper reports and editorials, magazine articles, cartoons and sketches. Into the tail end of a repressive century it came like the promise of a change in the weather, that unsettling notion that far from the troublesome corporeality of bodies being obscured by their enfolding layers of lawn and calico they might themselves become transparent, giving up their secrets to a gaze. By the summer of 1896 there were slot machines in Chicago that would X-ray your hand, and at that year's Electrical Exhibition in New York there was a tent in which the boxes stood one beside another in rows and people queued up to use them, the lines stretching backwards to the door. Afterwards, congregating in groups, talking in whispers as one might do in church, their eyes shone with the wonder of conversion and they said that during those few moments when they had seen their hands dissected on a screen they had received confirmation of their place among the living; or else they saw what Bertha Röntgen had done and in the peculiar repetitiveness of the images, each skeleton so like the last, they found the unindividuated mass of bones that we will all become. All through that year and the next, the enthralling mystery X-rays represented, their apparent promise, the sense they brought of a future already overtaken and inhabited, was such that when in Cedar Rapids, Iowa, a man claimed to have used X-rays to transmute base metal into gold, finding the philosopher's stone in a cathode-ray tube, for a while he was almost believed; and why not, since if a solid body might become transparent – if one might step inside a fairground booth and see the bones of one's own hand – if one might pay a dime and see one's life or death – then what after all might be possible, what understood – and surely this is what brought them, all that summer, running to the fairground booths: the promise of the simplifying power of explanation, sight: that knowing the constitution of their bodies they might be granted understanding of their minds.

Ten days after seeing my GP about my headaches, I went to the local hospital for an MRI scan. This hospital, tucked behind a busy road and hedged with bus stops, was nothing like the one I had so often visited with my mother, where well-tended gardens functioned as a euphemism does, to cushion and obscure, but was instead a vast and sprawling complex of concrete and peeling paint, its central portion grown incrementally outwards, extended and tacked on to as though it were trying to reproduce itself, scaffolding poles like aerial roots hanging from its walls and squat, shrub-like Portakabins sprouting from its car parks and what might once have been its lawns. Anxiety made me hurry as I walked into the main building's busy foyer but it took so long to find the right place that I was barely punctual by the time I presented myself at the MRI unit's reception desk. There I was given a sheaf of forms to fill in and directed to a corridor where half a dozen others sat already on plastic chairs lined up against both walls, each trying to keep as far from the others as they could. After a slight hesitation I picked a seat at the far end of the left-hand row next to a large man with a face which was badly swollen around its right eye, the skin about the socket stretched smooth, his eyebrow a muddled burr across a discoloured patch the size of a tangerine. Sitting down beside him, maintaining polite separation in this public space, I wished for a moment that instead of this withdrawal I might have the nerve to catch his gaze – but to do so would have been to pretend to a solidarity with him which I wasn't entitled to, because, after all, I was unlikely to be seriously ill, whereas he already had a slightly rotten look, his skin the flat, yellowish-white of sheep's cheese. We sat for nearly an hour, the pair of us, side by side, and all that time he remained unmoving apart from his thumbs, which he tapped gently and soundlessly against one another in a complicated rhythm I couldn't find the knack of, and I wondered if perhaps he was reciting some list or prayer in his head, a strengthening psalm or an accounting of all that stood to be lost; but when at last a nurse came and called him he stood up straight and square and greeted her with friendly courtesy, and so perhaps after all it had only been the waiting which had bothered him and my anxiously examined pity, my assumption that I must have what he did not – health, strength – and could therefore confer upon him with my glance some warmth of comfort, was only another form of conceit.

When my own turn came the same nurse led me further into the building, down corridors which smelled of linoleum and disinfectant and through a door into a tiny, white-walled cubicle where, left alone, I stripped off my clothes and put on instead a blue serge hospital gown, stiff from the laundry, its hemmed edges scratchy against the nape of my neck. My own things – my trousers and T-shirt, my shoes, the silver bracelet I wore all that year and my earrings and glasses – I placed in a locker; and so, stripped and blinded, it was as though I had been divested of all those complicated trappings which made me into myself, leaving nothing beyond them but the feature-less core; and I felt that I was approaching, not a routine medical examination, but some ritual of passage, a proof at last of all that constituted me. Another nurse came and took me into the room where the scanner was and I lay down on its waiting pallet, my head enclosed inside a frame, my knees raised on a cushion. Things were explained to me but without my glasses I found it hard to concentrate, the technician's words emerging indistinctly from a haze of colour. I was given a button to press in case claustrophobia should cause me to panic but without my glasses myopia had already enclosed me, cutting the comprehensible world down to a few inches of recognisable space, and I had no choice but to surrender, which was itself a relief after the months in which I had fought to keep myself in motion: here at last I was taken care of and might rest. Despite the headphones I had been given the volume of the machine's working was almost overwhelming, a roar of turning metal which occupied my skull, replacing thought with sound. I lost my sense of time and it began to feel as though I might have been fixed in that position, my head held in its cage, my knees on their pillow, for some elastic version of forever, and that I had reached at last a sort of crisis, a crux or an apotheosis after the months of anxious emptiness: that caught there, stuck inside an enormous white box, helpless and bare, I had become a pivot on which my life might turn; but afterwards, sat in the consultant's office with a picture of my brain spread out against a lightbox, I felt nothing. This was not how I had imagined it. I had thought that, seeing the illuminated image of that part of myself which was the keeper of the rest pinned up against a screen, the details of its operation picked out in nebulae of colour, I might know at last that I was solid, sure, and that I was well-made; and I had thought that I would recognise it, this invisible part of myself where consciousness resided, that I would know it was mine as an infant knows its mother, and that at last the understanding buried deep inside it would be made accessible, but this could have been a picture of anyone and I felt only a sort of dull surprise that what I saw should be a part of me at all. It told me nothing. I sat in my chair and listened patiently while the consultant explained that there was nothing obviously wrong with me – the scan was clear. I would be referred, she said, to a headache clinic, but there was a waiting list and in the interim I should continue with my routine of pain killers, avoid alcohol, try and sleep regularly; then, early the next year when the letter came with the time of my appointment, my headaches had gone. I had met Johannes. A shift had occurred and my mother's death was no longer present but past, its recalling an understanding of pattern instead of a wound, something woven into me, a part of that composite I had become which was a fraction of what I might have been; and this feat had been achieved not through understanding but only by familiarity of occupation, and by the passage of time.

II

When at last the long bell of my mother's death had ceased to sound, after the obliteration of her belongings in the skip and the scouring that my illness had been, after I had met Johannes, I felt for a long time that the past mattered very little. I lacked curiosity as much as I lacked material for it. My mother had been all that was left of my family and to accept the absolute nature of her loss, its insusceptibility to reconstruction through the careful husbanding of facts or objects, was almost a badge of honour. On those occasions when I thought about it at all, I considered myself to have done well in avoiding the temptation to become curator, the embalmer of my mother's memory. Even after my daughter was born – even after she had reached an age at which she showed interest when my mother's name was mentioned or when I saw how shadowy to her was the figure of this other grandmother, as distinct from Johannes' mother who was so pointedly alive, with her trips to the zoo and the national gallery, or to the Dutch church at Austin Friars – even then I felt little more

57

than inconvenienced by the need to traverse with my child such difficult territory as inherited grief. Trying to articulate it once to Johannes, explaining during one of those evenings in the first years of our daughter's life when she slept spread-eagled in her cot as though unconsciousness had assaulted her, knocking her out, while we lay next to one another on the sofa like the survivors of some localised disaster, I told him that the past is as prosaic as the future and the facts about it only so much stuff. To pick through dusty boxes, to sift through memories which fray and tear like ageing paper in an effort to find out who we are, is to avoid the responsibility of choice, since when it comes to it we have only ourselves, now, and the ever-narrowing cone of what we might enact. Growing up, I said, is a solitary process of disentanglement from those who made us and the reality of it cannot be avoided but only, perhaps, deferred – and my discarding of the physical mani-festation of the past, the emptying of my mother's house piece by piece into a rain-filled skip, had been a statement of intent and with it I had let myself be unencumbered—

—But you aren't,

Johannes said.

—You are not unencumbered.

My mother was an only child and my grandmother a psycho-analyst known to everyone, myself included, as Doctor K. This name didn't strike me as strange. It was to me only another part of the landscape of my childhood and I regarded it with solipsistic insularity, the assumption by one whose age is still in single figures that the world was what I saw of it and everything familiar was also ordinary, so that I was almost into my teens before I thought to ask her about it. We stood in her kitchen, the table between us and on it the knife that she had been using to chop vegetables, she having set this task aside so that she might offer my question the attention she believed that it deserved. This was a trick of hers: to treat conversation as an activity which should be given full attention, weighed against the virtue of silence, so that talking to her one might never have anywhere to hide one's face.

—Names,

she said

—are symbols. Particularly those we allocate to ourselves, and not knowing what to say in response I said nothing, but only stood and felt myself grow hot under her gaze until at last, satisfied, she picked up her knife again and went on with chopping carrots.

About my grandfather I know almost nothing. He was gone before my mother was born and left behind him little sense of absence, no space or lack, no mark to show how he might have fitted with us. On those occasions in childhood that I asked my mother about him, empty Saturday afternoons when I drifted bored about the house looking for threads to pull, she claimed to know only that he had worked at one of the journals that my grandmother contributed to and, if pressed, she would go to the large bookcase in the hall on which we kept our good books, the hardbacks and the row of old Penguins with their yellow spines, the classics in translation and the poetry, and she would take down a copy of the collected Kipling between whose fragile pages she kept a photograph of a man sat on a beach, a stretch of runnelled sand beyond which squat, grass-topped dunes rose to an indifferent sky. I don't know if the Kipling was a joke but

—There he is,

and she would pass the glossy sheet to me and go back to whatever she had been doing before my question interrupted her, leaving the book on the hall table to be refilled and replaced when I was done.

Calling this picture to mind now I place the man somewhere on the east coast, Thorpeness or Cromer, Snape – one of those long, flat beaches that separate the marshes of East Anglia from the uncompromising sea, places that Johannes and I go to sometimes, early in the autumn when the ground is warm but the air has a chill to it and when, in the late afternoons, the moon hangs like its own ghost in the sky and the reed-beds cast long shadows and everything is dusty, gold, and both of us are pierced, slightly and not unpleasantly, with a nostalgia for something that we have never seen but know, instinctively, that we have lost. The man in the photograph wore a pale-coloured shirt, open at the neck but awkwardly so, as though his tie had been discarded in a gesture of intentional carelessness, and his trousers were rolled up to show an inch of pale skin above gartered socks and laced brogues. His hair, disordered by the wind, framed a face that was little more than a smile and a squint, eyes screwed up against the sun, his features so indistinguishably ordinary that they seemed to me to approach disguise. Across the bottom of the picture the shadow of the photographer fell, clear and dark, and it is a peculiarity of the image as I remember it that there was more apparent character in this shadow – the body's black outline stretched across the sand, straight legs set apart, elbows raised like a first growth of sharply angled wings – than there was in the photograph's ostensible subject, the man who was my grandfather. This photo I lost years ago – abandoned, presumably, with the Kipling, cast off to become someone else's curiosity, the sort of thing that turns up from time to time in books bought second-hand, but I remember how at the time I studied it with absolute attention, gazing at it with my nose inches from its surface. Picking at its details, I tried to find anything in it that might prove its connection to myself; but he could have been anybody's grandfather, that man, and I wonder now if in fact the photograph had anything to do with us at all or if, rather, it came as it went, sandwiched between the verses of 'Gunga Din'. It seems unlikely that my mother knew as little about her father as she claimed. Doctor K's honesty was scrupulous, her determination that one must not hide from facts nor shirk the task of interpreting them verging, at times, on aggression. In response my mother had become pragmatic. She prioritised outcome over fact and she was not above lying, feeling, I think, that by doing so she was protecting both her own privacy and mine, the right I had to understand the world as I chose. It seems so obvious now that I wonder how I hadn't seen it before: that my mother's professed ignorance on the subject of her father was her own invention. Such an equivocation would have seemed to her no more than expedient, this judicious husbanding of complicated trivia a way of shielding me from something which she thought unimportant; and after all what difference is there between an honestly told untruth and a lie: our understanding of a past we didn't inhabit will always be a fiction. To say that I might have had a right to truth would have seemed, to my mother, absurd, so that even if I had recognised this fabrication before her death and found a way to ask about it, the question rising through those empty tracts of space that filled the house as illness abraded her, then still I don't think she would have seen any reason to answer.

In the afternoons Johannes takes our daughter out and I lie with my feet up on a cushion and try to rest, my body an uncomfortable object to inhabit. My hips ache. The baby kicks. My fingers thicken and are unwieldy; the doing or undoing of buttons is a chore. At such times, wishing the lot of them gone – Johannes, the children both inside me and out – I wonder what they will keep of me, later; what off-cut memories will remain to be re-stitched, their resemblance to myself a matter of perspective. I want only what I think we all must want: to come off as better than I ought, more generous, more sure – kinder than I know myself to be; but I want also to be known, to be counted and to be excused. I can't have both. The thought of it makes me surly and resentful and when the baby knees me in the ribs I snap at it through the intermediary layers of my flesh; and later, guilty, I hold my daughter close and sing to her as though I might with such tendernesses obliterate her recollection of all the times I haven't come quite up to scratch.

My grandmother lived on the upper floors of a large house in Hampstead, the heath rising like a city's dream of English countryside beyond the end of its long garden. She had bought the house, dilapidated then, the year that she turned thirty, shortly after qualifying as a psychoanalyst, and since then she had slowly reworked it, fitting its rooms around herself, until she seemed to sit within it like a stone inside its setting. Except in the attic, which had been her childhood bedroom, there was no trace of my mother: no photographs, no mementos. Such things had no place in those high-ceilinged rooms from which emotion had been smoothed to leave reason, the salve, behind. The house's basement had been converted, shortly after my mother had left home, into a separate flat, a source of income which insulated Doctor K from the fear of growing old, and for as long as I could remember it was occupied by a former patient, a very upright ex-schoolteacher who wore tweed suits smelling of peppermint and camphor, and seemed to live in a perpetual state of just-held-back decay. Often during the month-long holiday that I spent there each summer, while Doctor K saw clients, I would go and sit with him on the stone terrace that ran along the back of the house, separating it from the garden, and which was his to use, French windows opening onto it from his living room. These are a child's memories perfected by adulthood's glaze and in them the days were always hot, the sky blue, and the garden stretched out, private, perfect in the dappled light which fell through the leaves of the over-hanging apple tree. The tenant made me cups of sweetened tea and we were companionable. He told me how my grand-mother had cured him, years earlier, of a form of compulsive self-harm which had driven him, over the course of several years, to pull out all the hair on his head and face by the roots. Now he spent his days growing roses, and I would watch him, his fingers deep amongst the leaves, checking for greenfly. Often he would stop what he was doing and stand for minutes on end staring at nothing, his arms loose at his sides and his head bowed down towards the ground, as though he had been momentarily uncoupled from himself, and at such times I would feel pity for him and this feeling, hot and uncomfort-able, would send me running back towards the house.

In the same way that it was always hot and the garden always very green, in my memories of the summers that I spent there my grandmother's house was always cool and always very quiet, a muted and a peaceful place where one might sit in comfort between the bookcases and feel that an escape had been effected. It was not a house that welcomed children. Its rooms had the same authoritative calm that university librar-ies possess – knowledge both offered and assumed, with learn-ing the price for further learning – and it conferred on me, for the duration of my stay, a sort of precocious adulthood. I enjoyed it, the graceful shapes my body made in the armchairs, the way I walked along the corridors with steady steps, the free rein I had amongst the books. My grandmother granted me autonomy. Staying there I might do as I liked, going out alone to watch the kite fliers on Parliament Hill or swim in the bathing ponds, taking a picnic with me that I had made myself, and I was responsible for brushing my own hair and teeth, for choosing appropriate shoes and taking a coat or not, and if I got wet then it was my own fault; but I was a child still and when I came home shivering my grandmother wouldn't run a bath as my mother would have done, or wrap me in a blanket to warm me through, making disapproval of a piece with care, and when I fell and grazed my knees it was my own hands that peeled the plaster from its plastic backing and stuck it, bloody, to my skin.

In the morning when our daughter wakes, Johannes goes to her and opens up her bedroom blinds. He takes her to the bathroom, sits her on the toilet, makes her wash her hands. He finds breakfast, bowls of porridge or slices of toast which the two of them eat together at the table. When it is time for Johannes to work I dress and go downstairs and I do the washing up while my daughter nags at me to read her a story. I fold laundry. I think about what to have for lunch. When we go out I make sure that my daughter's shoes are on the right feet, I check the bag for water and spare pants. I take her hand. We go to the park or we sit on the upper decks of buses and travel to the places that she likes: the library where she can pretend

65

to work at the computers, the museum with a rocking horse on which she can take turns. We do the shopping. She chooses her own fruit, apples or nectarines, and is allowed to eat some of it on the way home, juice smeared across her face and down her neck. In the evenings, after Johannes has come down from his office, we sit together, all three of us, and talk about the days we've had and sometimes we are happy and sometimes we are tired and cross and each minute is an effort of patience. We make dinner. We put our child to bed. This is what routine is like, or love.

Each year on the first Saturday of August my mother and I would walk past the post office and the pub, past the primary school and the supermarket to the station and, leaving suburbia behind, would take the train into London and, changing at Waterloo, the Tube to Hampstead, whose broad streets sat above the city, looking down. As we came in sight of my grandmother's house we would see her waiting for us, standing at the kitchen window dressed in evening clothes, a long, full skirt with a narrow waist and a high-necked blouse, a cameo brooch pinned to her throat, her hair in its tight wave and, walking in and out of the shadows that the plane trees cast across the pavement, I would feel my mother's fingers tighten round my own, as though she were afraid that I might run away from her and that I would be lost.

By the time we reached the steps which led from the small front garden with its clay-tiled path up to my grandmother's front door she would be there to welcome us and, stepping forward, would take us each in turn by the shoulders and would kiss us twice, two evenly placed markers, one on either cheek; and then I would be sent upstairs with my suitcase to the small room Doctor K kept for me through the eleven months that elapsed between each of my visits. This room was in the attic, reached by a staircase whose narrow steps, rising awkwardly away from the rest of the house, were tucked in behind a brass-handled door opposite Doctor K's bedroom. It smelled differently to the rooms on the lower floors, a musty scent like long-stored wool, and often, closing the staircase door behind me, I felt as though I were leaving the house altogether and entering a space that was both separate and my own, and each evening this came as a relief, tension leeching away from me with every ascended step. This room lacked the restrained beauty which made the rest of the house seem so much like a stage. The furniture was tatty, old: an iron bedstead, very high off the ground, its mattress covered in a patchwork quilt; an armchair upholstered in velvet, much faded and scratched; a chest of drawers with a cracked walnut veneer. Around a two-paned dormer window looking out across the roof and the garden towards the heath, the room's whitewashed ceiling sloped towards a floor whose boards were covered in overlapping rugs, many of them with their naps worn through to leave bare patches of pale-coloured warp. I loved this room very much and still, at times, I wish that I could go back to it, to feel myself both above and alone. Before I was born it had been my mother's, and the white-painted bookshelf which leaned fifteen degrees west of true was still filled with books which had once been hers. Sometimes, opening them, I would disturb loose sheets of paper that fluttered downwards, drifting to the floor to settle gently amongst the swirling patterns of the rugs, disjointed lists of words, phone numbers or addresses or single pages cut from longer letters, descriptions of nameless places, congratulations on achievements since forgotten. I would pick them up and hold them and, trying to connect their recipient with my mother, so uncompromisingly grown up, so firm and sure, I would catch from the corner of my eye the outline of my own inescapable adulthood flicker against the yellowed walls, a long shadow cast by a low sun.

After I had unpacked, putting my own books alongside my mother's on the shelf, filling the chest of drawers with my clothes, laying out my pyjamas on the pillow, I would go back downstairs to find Doctor K trimming runner beans at the kitchen table while, in the living room, my mother sat quite upright in an armchair, a gin and tonic and a bowl of crisps on the little table beside her.

—Have you unpacked?

she would ask, and

—Have you washed your hands?

and when I said that I had done both she would tell me to go and find my grandmother and ask her if she needed help but, trailing into the kitchen to do as I was told, my grandmother would tell me not to get under her feet, and often during those first evenings, uncertain of my place, I would sit outside in the hall, folded up across the span of the staircase's bottom step, listening to the murmur of the radio spill out with the scent of garlic through the kitchen door.

For three days we remained in such uneasy equilibrium. Each morning I would come down to the kitchen where Doctor K stood, arranging my mother's breakfast on a tray, fresh croissants from the bakery split and spread with jam, and next to them a small pot of coffee and a jug of milk. I was not allowed to visit my mother in her room. My own breakfast was eaten in the kitchen and Doctor K insisted that I stayed downstairs until my mother had dressed, and then, during the morning, Doctor K would give me chores, laying out newspaper on the kitchen table and setting me to clean candlesticks, the damp wadding from a can of Brasso turning my fingers black while outside in the garden my mother lay on a rug, reading, and after lunch my mother was sent back to her room to rest while I was turned out onto the heath. At the time I regarded these separations as an unnecessary affront and I thought my grandmother excessive, my mother frail for giving in, because I took for granted that she resented them as much as I did. It is only now that I can see these few days for what they were: my grandmother's only way of taking care, my mother's only way of being cared for, this exchange effected silently while we all pretended to be occupied elsewhere. I did what I could to undermine them. Given the opportunity I would escape my grandmother's planned occupations and run into the garden to lie next to my mother on the rug, pulling up grass by the roots and knowing that now I had won through

I would be allowed to stay with my mother for the rest of the day. Doctor K would come out into the garden, hands smoothing out the creases in her skirt, and she would tell me that I must go indoors but

—Let her stay,

my mother said, and wrapped her arms around me. With a child's unhesitating cruelty I made my mother choose and, as if to emphasise the strength of her decision, on those reclaimed afternoons we would go out, up to the brightly painted shops in Hampstead Village, and she would buy me things – lawn cotton dresses or handwash-only cardigans, brightly coloured sandals, kites of Japanese paper stretched across a bamboo frame or soft-haired dolls too delicate for play – things to be coveted rather than owned; and afterwards I would clutch the loaded bags to my chest and we would sit and drink lemonade in front of one of the pavement cafes. This was the closest that I ever felt to her, I think; but I felt too as though in the winning of proximity something had been dismantled which had kept me sheltered. Love, for my mother, was not distinct from action. For years she had been putting into practice the contention that we exist, not as icebergs do, nine-tenths hidden and the visible portion no more than a poor clue to the greater, deeper bulk below, but at the surface, spread out along our planes of intersection; and now for an afternoon we had replaced this solid surety of position with something else and, perched above London with our parcels, I felt the lack of it.

*

Throughout the early stages of her illness I assumed that at some point in her dying the barrier between my mother and myself would be breached, no longer being necessary, and that through it some manner of truth would spill, coming as a trickle or a flood to engulf us and to wash us clean. I assumed that I would be granted access at last to those parts of her life which, throughout my childhood, had been kept meticulously separate from me, their presence felt but unmentioned, surrounding me as though I were a visitor to a house with half its rooms unseen, and that at last I would be able to walk through them, these stores for all the private tat and trivia of thought which makes a person both fragile and themselves. I assumed, then, that in the end I would take ownership of this as I would of all the rest of it, the house, the garden – a matter of legality, a process of inheritance in which preference had no part. Through those last long months, though, the physical intimacy which her illness demanded of us left no space for any more metaphorical form of contact – the present was too onerous to allow any intrusion by the past, and the work of being kind, against the urge to hurt which comes as vulnerability's unwelcome companion, left no energy for confession. The only times that we ever hovered close to revelation were on those afternoons in Hampstead. Then my mother would talk about herself as if she were someone else, a person whose life was meat for speculation, and she would talk about Doctor K, so that at times I could glimpse an otherwise unapprehended truth: that they were not what I had taken adults to be, each a finished entity, but rather were still in progress, and that

71

they too were a mother and a daughter, tied to one another. Once, after we had drunk our lemonade and paid the bill, as we walked slowly back towards Doctor K's house carrying the purchases whose extravagance already shamed us, my mother told me how, each morning during childhood, she would sit at the scrubbed table in the Hampstead kitchen, surrounded by the toast crumbs and the jam pots, the teacups' dregs, while my grandmother asked her about her dreams, questioning her in detail about their content; and that because of this, by the time my mother was five or six years old, she had stopped dreaming entirely. Afterwards I wished she hadn't told me. The thought of my mother as a child, her dreams jettisoned as though they were no more than empty wrappers, chilled me. All through the evening I avoided talking and at dinner I hunched over my plate as though it were a penance until my grandmother said I must be coming down with something, and sent me up to bed, where I lay, miserable, all through the fading evening, a jumper over my nightdress, an extra blanket from the bottom of the chest of drawers wrapped round my shoulders, wondering how often knowledge comes like this: a casually effected violence which throws the world just west of true.

After three days my mother left, returning to that quiet analogue of her life in which I was absent, trying in the earlier years to repair her relationship with my father and later to recover from it, and then I would feel the guilty lightening of relief like an unacknowledgeable weight removed.

Released from the entangling strictures of a relationship I didn't understand I felt as though I had run a swift course into open water and, alone for the remainder of the month with Doctor K, left largely to my own devices, I felt myself free. During the greater part of every day my grandmother worked; I learned to keep doors closed, to leave no personal possessions in the hallway that led past the kitchen and the study to her consulting room – learned, too, to retreat to some deeper portion of the house between five to and five past every hour, those ten minutes during which one client left and another arrived, sitting round the bend in the stairs so that I could listen to the sound that two shadows made sliding past one another and trying to imagine from the sound their footsteps made on the hallway's wooden boards the details of these incomprehensibly other lives. On hot days when the windows were open and voices carried clearly, the walls of the house responding like a sounding board, I would find myself occasionally startled by the noise of weeping or by a shout, its echoes deadened by the still air of the summer garden.

At the start of each day – after the breakfast things had been cleared and the floor swept, the papers straightened on the hall table, the mirror that hung above it wiped; those minutiae which, attended to, transformed the lower floor of the flat from habitation to a refuge for paying strangers – Doctor K hung a laminated sign on the door of her consulting room on which the words *Analysis in Progress* were written in heavy-inked, formal lettering. This, said Doctor K, when I complained

that it was unnecessary given that I knew better than to inter-
rupt, was not for my benefit, being used even when, as was
more usual, there was no one else in the flat. Rather it was a
part of the ritual of analysis, a formal acknowledgement of the
pact that she made to be available as absolutely as she was able
for the time that she had allotted to those who came to visit
her, climbing with what combination of anticipation and anxiety I could not imagine five or six times a week up the stairs
from the street. Doctor K was always ready to explain to me
the mechanics of her profession, taking my questions more
seriously than I ever intended them to be. At such times she
would treat me as a sort of proto-adult, stopping what she was
doing to speak, and, flattered, I would try hard to concentrate,
although lack of comprehension made it difficult, her words
slipping past while I squinted to catch the shape of them. I
didn't doubt the truth of what she said. I assumed, then, that
knowledge was synonymous with fact – that understanding
must bring with it certainty so that, knowing, one would know
for sure; and such surety I looked forward to, taking it to be a
part of adulthood which would come, at last, when I had
earned it.

Left to my own devices for the greater part of each day, I
spent most of my time reading and I was happy, if this is what
happiness is, this tendency to be engrossed, an enthusiasm
for the drowning out of thought with words; and then each
evening, when Doctor K's last client had left, she would come
and find me. This was the only time that I was allowed into
her consulting room: when, for half an hour each evening

74

before dinner, we would sit in there together, in a pair of facing armchairs set beneath the window. The room was large and its windows looked, as those of the living room did, out across the garden. It seemed always to be cool, even when hot days stretched on for hours, and it had that kind of heavy, impenetrable quiet which I have since come to associate with National Trust properties: the peace of things that are not used, that are curated, precisely placed, unmoved and untouched by those who pass through. The floor was lime-washed wood, pale and clean, covered for the most part by a large red-and-purple Persian carpet, and besides the two chairs on which Doctor K and I sat, and the bookcases that lined three walls of the room from the floor to a foot off the ceiling, and which housed all Doctor K's psychoanalytic books, the only furniture was a bureau and a couch, a long, low ottoman upholstered in velvet faded to the washed-out brownish green of a shadowed pond. This couch, low-backed and piled with cushions at one end, I was not allowed to sit on, it being imbued, or so I inferred from the way that Doctor K spoke about it, with some power of compulsion, a mysterious tendency to induce in its occupants a time-consuming and uncheckable catharsis. As a result it became an object of desire for me. I tried to imagine the drama of myself upon it, how I would be laid out, wan and troubled, words dropping from my lips like the fruit of a slow-grown bush, but could only think how awkward it would be to sit on its edge, mute and uncomfortable, and how the thought of lying there while someone watched me would bring panic like the fear of drowning. Often, while Doctor K was absent from the flat, when she walked to the bakery or went on Wednesday evenings to play bridge at the house of the elderly pianist who lived on the top floor of the house opposite, I would stand in my bare feet outside the closed door of the consulting room and try to work up the courage to go inside, daring myself to approach the couch, to lower myself onto it; but if I ever did then I have no recollection of it, and nor do I know what happened to the couch after Doctor K's death. I imagine that my mother would have sold it if she could, as she sold all the books, not to turn a profit but because she was pragmatic and disliked waste; or if it couldn't be sold she would have thrown it away as she did the heavy consulting room carpet which, when we lifted a corner of it on the day after the funeral, both of us seeking a way to occupy ourselves in the solitary vacuum that comes when death's formalities are complete, we found to be so riddled with moths that, disturbed, they flew up in clouds and the carpet began to shred and fall into grainy dust in our hands.

For that half an hour in the consulting room each evening, between the end of Doctor K's working day and the start of dinner, which we cooked together, her standing over the hob while I sat at the kitchen table chopping potatoes or shredding spring onions for a salad, we sat and faced one another. Through the open window drifted the gentle roar of traffic climbing Haverstock Hill, and mixed in with it the calling voices of people turned out into the freedom of the heath's open spaces, but we were close together and very far from them and all these outside noises came to us as though through swaddling layers of cloth. Throughout the time that we sat there my grandmother maintained a sort of listening stillness, sat upright and unmoving, her feet crossed at the ankle and her hands in her lap, her eyes focused on me as I fidgeted about and tried, without alerting her to what I was doing, to catch sight of the dial of the watch she wore on the inside of her wrist. Her face was not expressionless but nor did it convey any particular emotion and she gave the impression not of waiting, which would have implied expectation, but rather of an impartial readiness, as though she would attend to anything that might be said but would be equally content to remain as she was, sat in silence, until the seven o'clock chime from the grandfather clock in the hall set us free. On the deep windowsill which stretched between the two chairs sat two corresponding glasses, a gin for Doctor K and for me a glass of lemonade browned with angostura bitters, their outsides sweating, their ice cubes melting slowly in the cool room. These drinks, said Doctor K, were further indicators, like not using the couch and no sign pinned up outside the door, that we were not in consultation. It was, she said, no kind of analysis that we were conducting, a point which she said needed to be emphasised more for her own benefit than for mine, as it was she who had its habit and routines ingrained. Rather than analysis, she said, this was an opportunity for us to talk without any mediating activity. It was an opportunity for reflection. She told me that without reflection, without the capacity to trace our lives backwards and pick the patterns out, we become liable to act as animals do, minus forethought and according to a set of governing laws which we have never taken the trouble to explore. Without reflection we do little more than drift upon the surface of things and self-determination is an illusion. We lay ourselves open to unbalance. Conversation, she said, helps us to reflect – and although much of what Doctor K said to me I at first failed to understand and then came to doubt, this point I have come back to; and I think that had I remembered it during those lost and lonely months after my mother's death when the contents of my mind were a formless spread that I could neither abandon nor inhabit, then perhaps things might have been easier for me.

At the time I found these evening talks with my grandmother uncomfortable, a fact that she acknowledged but which, she said, was an indication only that we were engaged in something valuable, as though my discomfort were a call sign, something to be sought and followed. Although for the most part I was little more than bored, there were times when I felt myself trapped. Reticence was no protection. Doctor K was as able to find significance in my silence as in my speech and any act of concealment would itself be considered revelatory. I felt that in the steady light of Doctor K's compassionate gaze my body, far from being the container and concealer of my mind, had become its compulsive betrayer and I wished that instead of entering the consulting room we might go straight to the easy companionship of dinner's preparation when, stood side by side, otherwise engaged, we might talk in fragments, about what I was reading or what I had seen, about Doctor K's friends or her tangential recollections of a childhood that seemed impossibly distant to me then and more so now. Under such conditions, through such circum-locutions, I felt that what was important could be admitted, unsaid but understood; but lately I have found that some version of Doctor K's routine has returned to me. Each even-ing, after our daughter is asleep, surrounded by the chaos made from our once-ordered lives, Johannes and I sit together for half an hour and let our thoughts unwind in silence or in fractured sentences, this ritual proximity an attempt to touch one another across a widening space of tiredness and habit, and although we do not confess, are neither priests nor penitents, still it is a kind of undressing and we are better for it.

This was Doctor K's contention: that the formal work of psychoanalysis, the daily meeting of analyst and analysand, should not be thought of as the elucidation of a person directly but rather as the teaching by example of a skill which, once learned, might be practised internally. It is, she said, easy to see analysis as a kind of laying out, a mental correlate of that physical ordering which occurs after death: the contents of a person unpacked and spread across the patterned surface of the Persian carpet, each artefact itemised, assessed; and then, inventory made, these objects put away again, more neatly now, their relations to one another drawn and understood; but minds repacked will tend, she said, to chaos, with more stuff shoved in lazily on top, the whole swiftly deteriorating into the same shifting mess it started as.

—It is a common mistake,

Doctor K told me, her hands lifting slightly from her lap in a gesture of emphasis that I cannot think would have been unconscious

—to think of the process in such passive terms.

These conversations – in which my part, if any, was that of unwilling interlocutor, my questions heavily prompted by my grandmother – took place not in the consulting room, where the spontaneous nature of what speech I chose to make was sacrosanct, but in any otherwise unoccupied corners of our days, on Sunday afternoons when it was hot and we would sit out on the lawn, Doctor K in a wicker chair and me on the grass in front of her, or in the evenings, after we had watched together some drama or documentary on the brown, wood-laminate television set that she kept in a small study next to her bedroom, until illness robbed her of the use both of the stairs and the evening hours. The analyst, Doctor K told me, is not a tour guide, leading their client through those vast and vaulted galleries, the cloisters of the mind, and nor is it their task to point out shadows, but rather they must provide an instruction in the mechanics of such shadows' investigation. It is only, she told me – each summer a different form of words, each summer the branches of the apple trees which grew espaliered against the garden fence a little longer, my

80

legs a little longer on the sofa – when a person has gained the skills necessary to explore the territory for themselves, to unpack their own minds and begin to understand the contents, that they might start the work necessary to make their experience, their behaviour meaningful; and then at last they might start to become transparent to themselves. This, she said, was the original significance of her name, adopted when she was young enough not to find such gestures awkward and kept to since as a way of keeping faith with herself: to mark herself as her life's subject, a case study in which she was both analyst and analysand, carried on across decades in an attempt to peel away the obscuring layers, the muddying cross-currents of desire, and to live a life which was intentional, directed not by the hidden motivations of a covered mind but by an elucidated self. Her first client, each morning, was herself, and for fifty minutes she would sit at the bureau in her consulting room and write in one of the large, leather-backed notebooks that she kept for the purpose an account of the previous day's events, her reactions to them, her dreams or reveries; and then she would read back through what she had written and annotate it with the same interpretations she would provide for any other subject. This diary keeping was, she said, not strictly necessary to the task of self-analysis but it was a methodology which she found useful, a way of holding the mind to task, like the use of a rosary in prayer. When, the summer that I was nine or ten, I tried to outgrow my childhood through mimicry, I kept for a while my own imitation of my grandmother's diary. We went together on a Saturday afternoon to the bookshop at the bottom of the hill, and there my grandmother bought me a smaller version of the notebook that she used and a good pen to go with it, and returning to her flat we moved, between us, a small table to sit beneath the window in my bedroom and in front of it a little round-backed chair. I laid out the notebook and set the pen next to it and the next morning, after breakfast, while my grandmother sat in her consulting room, I sat at the table and tried to write. After ten minutes or so I had managed a list of everything achieved the previous day and given as much thought as I was able to the significance of it. The dormer window was open and I could hear the scratching and cooing of the pigeons who nested on the roof. At the bottom of the page I had been writing on I drew a picture of a witch. After a while I climbed onto the table and stuck my head out of the window to see if I could catch sight, from up here, of any hint of a bald spot in the downstairs tenant's hair as he stood in front of a bed of roses with a pair of secateurs held loosely in his hand.

Later, as we sat together in the kitchen over a lunch of ham sandwiches, I felt an inner swell of importance as I waited for Doctor K to ask me how I had got on. All morning, after the tedious execution of the task itself had been got out of the way, I had been imagining what I would say when asked about my diary. Concerned more with an image of myself as diary keeper than with the actual act of writing I was eager to have an opportunity to demonstrate this new facet to my personality; but Doctor K made no mention of it. Even when the next morning, as we cleared away the breakfast things, I loudly announced my intention to go to my room and work and then, half mounting the stairs, turned back to look at her, she did nothing more than nod. It puzzles me still, this peculiar idea of privacy Doctor K had, that all my thoughts and actions, my hidden wants, the ripples of my mind across my face, my skin, should be considered little more than symptom while the act of examination itself was sacrosanct.

Despite the difficulty in its actual execution I held to the idea of diary writing for the rest of the month, keeping faith with my morning retreat to the table beneath the window, and when my holiday was over and I returned home I made my mother clear out a space for me in the box room, sorting through years of accumulated junk until I could fit a chair in there and an old writing bureau she bought at my insistence from a junk shop, and I made a sign to be pinned up on the door. I wonder now if this was some feint on my part, a testing of the waters, to see how it would feel to ally myself to Doctor K, and whether perhaps this was the year that I came to understand, if not what held my mother and my grandmother apart, then at least the presence of their separation. That my mother carried out my instructions without comment or question despite the fact that it must have irritated her was, I think, a testament to her patience, but it was sensible too, because the feeling of importance that it gave me to retreat each morning before school to the box room and hang up the sign and shut the door soon wore off, and I found other ways to entertain myself. The box room drifted back to being a repository for odds and ends of household rubbish, for ironing boards and baskets and spare sheets, for jumpers in need of mending and chairs with broken legs or backs – those things we couldn't use but couldn't bring ourselves to throw away; and upon all this its door could be shut, granting us the illusion of a house in order. And when, years later, after my mother's death, I came to sort through it all again, to disinter object after half-discarded object from the softening dust which lay across the room, each one become through disuse little more than an imitation of itself, I found at the back of the room the bureau and, on it, the leather notebook, neatly placed, the pen set parallel beside it. The notebook I kept, saving it from the skip because it felt a part of me, vestigial but somehow still adjoining, and I expect that it is somewhere in this house now although I couldn't say precisely where, a part of that silted edifice, built in layers, which is my own paper carcass, a repository the sorting of which will be my children's task. My grandmother's notebooks she destroyed as soon as she found out that she was dying, spending an hour each afternoon between naps and medication feeding them methodically through a shredder. They had been, she said, a tool for her analysis and not its outcome, that outcome being, depending on your point of view, either the articles she had written over forty years explaining and defending her project and its method, or her life itself – what she had made of it, its worm-cast trail – but more, her own experience of it, that inner life which, so long laboured over, would soon be lost.

*

84

After my mother told me that she had ceased to dream I began to find myself lying awake, in my bedroom at home or during the summer in the room at the top of Doctor K's house, when I should have been asleep – not every night, but maybe once or twice a fortnight. Partly it was a sudden awareness of my own sleeping patterns which disrupted them – the way that, thinking about my mother and the mechanics of her dream-lessness, I would lie with my eyes shut, trying to notice the point at which dreams began – but partly also it was the preoccupying strangeness of it, those dark, imageless hours between sleeping and waking. Having learned the fact I kept it as a curiosity, taking it out during my own solitary night-lit hours to turn it this way and that, trying to make sense of it – this single artefact I had of my mother's existence apart from myself. At home in the mornings I would sit, tired, my school uniform half-buttoned, on the tall stool in the corner of the kitchen and watch my mother slot bread into the toaster, boil the kettle, reach down a pot of jam from the high shelf in the cupboard where it lived because at one time I had liked to put my fingers in it when her back was turned, and I would feel that, despite the familiarity of these gestures, despite the known quantity of her face and the predictability of her responses to me, the woman I was watching was a stranger; but surely this cannot have been the case. The truth must be that I knew my mother well because, after all, what are we if not a totality of days, a sum of interactions; and a glimpse of what is underneath the surface, the skeleton on which the outer face is hung, cannot undo the knowledge of

85

skin but only give it context, the way it rises and falls, its puckering, its flaws.

One particular summer, sometime between sports day and my French exam, my father left at last, his presence, always tentative, often forgotten, finally ceasing altogether. My parents sat side by side in our sitting room to tell me what I had failed to notice – that my father had gone – and I thought only how unusual it was that we should be all three in the same room. Later, when my mother came to my bedroom to ask if there was anything more that I wanted to know, I could think of nothing to say. It seemed that nothing tangible had happened and that afterwards things went on as before. Term ended. The long holiday began. My father came and went without warning so that, as I had always done, I assumed his absence, tried not to seem resentful of his presence. For a few weeks I wandered from one friend's house to another while my mother worked, and then my bags were packed and we made the journey to Doctor K's. My mother stayed for the weekend, and if Doctor K tried less hard to keep us apart than was usual, if I spent more time sat by mother's side, then I barely noticed it; and then my mother left, and I was alone with my grandmother and the flat and the heath. The weather that year was indifferent, grey and rather humid, and when I climbed to the top of Parliament Hill in the afternoons there was a pollution haze spread out across the eastward city like a caul; or perhaps this is another trick that memory plays, to point and dramatise: the addition of an appropriate backdrop for the mood. I found myself distractible, easily bored, and I seemed to have no handle on what I felt: although I would not have said that I was unhappy small things distressed me without warning. One evening, towards the end of the first week, I sat in Doctor K's consulting room and wept because I had been unable to reach my father by phone, and although this was not unusual, although he would not have been expecting me to call and so would have had no reason to stay near a phone, although it had been nothing more than a whim which had led me to dial his number and I could think of nothing that I wanted to say to him, still I felt as though my failure to reach him was a suddenly effected, ragged wound. Doctor K poured our drinks and we sat in our usual chairs. Surrounded by the room's familiar comfort, I was surprised by my own desolation, which came as a longing not just for my own home but for my mother, or for what my mother would have done to treat my unhappiness, tending to it as though it were a fever or a graze, susceptible to the same rules of comfort as any other injury: a bath, hot milk, a kiss; those simplicities which, treating sorrow as a fact in itself, require no act of explanation on the part of one already wounded.

Doctor K:

—It is important that we talk about these things.

My mother, when she asked me how I felt about my father leaving, had offered no platitudes but left instead the complicated state of things arrayed about us like the wreckage of an ocean voyage as we sat, survivors, side by side on the edge of my bed; and if I had any questions beyond the purely logistical I knew better than to ask them.

Doctor K:

—Would you like to tell me how you feel?

I sat in the chair opposite my grandmother, curled over on myself as though to protect an injury to my front or flank, unstopped tears running down my face to wet the knees of my summer trousers, and I shut my eyes so that I would not have to look beneath the surface of things.

Doctor K:

—Sometimes if we are angry with someone we love, it doesn't feel acceptable to us and so we find other places to put that anger.

Doctor K:

—We might think we are angry with someone else instead.

My mother, as she talked, had held my hand.

Doctor K:

—Or we might feel very sad.

Across the empty acres of the consulting room carpet, Doctor K's words reached me; but for all the promise implicit in the act of talking we did not touch and I was not comforted.

In my last year at university, sat one evening in my room eating an indifferent vegetable curry for the third night running, two pairs of socks protecting my feet from the cold, and through the window a view of the chapel lit up against the darkness in a way that never failed to make me feel mildly, half-pleasantly bereft, I read for the first time Freud's account of the psychoanalysis of a four-year-old boy, Little Hans. Although during each of the Augusts that I had spent at my grandmother's house I had done little but read, having nowhere to go except the heath, nor any friends nearby, and although I had been given more or less free rein of the books in the house, allowed my own pick of what was on the shelves, still I had never read any psychoanalysis. Those books relating to her work my grandmother kept in her consulting room, and although not strictly forbidden them I would never have felt myself able, while she sat and watched, to run my fingers along their spines as I did with those in the rest of the house, waiting for something to catch my attention. Even now, so long afterwards, the thought of what my grandmother's response would have been, her enthusiasm, the opportunity she would have seen to teach, brings an immediate and indivisible firmness of response: the automatic certainty that I must allow my grandmother no ingress to my mind beyond what she had already granted to herself. Then, after her death, the books were gone; and with an adolescent's callousness I didn't think about my grandmother for a long time, or about the past, or anything but my own life and how I might get on with it. Now, though, reading the slightly stilted prose of a decades-old translation of Freud's case studies, I felt my childhood spread about me like a map to which I had almost learned the key, and for days afterwards I felt myself to be a little out of focus, as though I had been away somewhere and had yet to complete the process of my return. As I walked to lectures or to the library, or sat drinking weak coffee in the college bar, I found myself haunted by the thought of Herbert Graf, anonymised by Freud as Little Hans, who at the age of four and three quarters saw a horse fall down in the street and afterwards became so frightened that he couldn't leave the house. His subsequent analysis was carried out primarily by his father, Max, with Freud offering support by letter – an extension of a process that was already in place, since Freud had for some time been encouraging those of his supporters who had young children to observe and report on their development, seeking in this way to gain confirmation of his theories of childhood sexuality. Freud himself would meet Herbert only once during the course of his analysis, on the afternoon of 30 March 1908 when the three of them – Herbert and his father and *Herr Doktor,* Freud – would sit in Freud's consulting room, awkwardly arrayed on chairs about the empty couch, Herbert's small-boy body uncomfortably still while – perhaps – from elsewhere in the apartment the sounds of freer children filtered through. Herbert was a polite, good-natured boy who tried hard to please, giving the best answers he could to questions he barely understood. Freud asked him if the horses that he was afraid of wore glasses; he said they didn't. Freud asked him if his father Max wore glasses and, confused, the boy said no to this as well although it wasn't true. Freud asked him if what he had described as the black around the mouths of the horses that frightened him might be a moustache; and Herbert, hands clasped between his knees, said he supposed it might. It was not, the eminent professor told him, horses that he was afraid of. Nor, as his father had suggested to him, was his anxiety mere synecdoche, the whole of the dreaded animal standing in for its penis. His fear, Freud said, was of his father; and Herbert, just turned five, who had seen a horse fall down and felt the safety of his bounded world eroded, sat quietly, and tried to see how this was true. His fear, for all its power, had previously been a simple thing, susceptible to adult protection; now he was being asked to put in place of it a metastasising complexity – an enforced awareness of the unreliability of thought, the way that one thing can come to stand in for another without us noticing the difference. Even now I feel the horror of it: to be made to feel in ignorance of oneself, to be stripped of those privileges subjectivity brings – a still, sure place to stand; a premise; the right to know one's mind – and I think of them walking home together, Herbert and his father, hurrying back through busy streets towards the safety of home, the boy whose trust had been opened like a nut, split to see what mechanism it was that made it grow, falling into step beside his analyst father, who far from being the negation of fear was now its subject; and I can think only of how thin the world must have seemed to him, how fragile – what had been that morning a presumed certainty made now into something like a body of water, the taut surface on which they walked a meagre miracle stretched across its depths.

My mother lay in her bed, a barrow's shape beneath the sheets, her hair, lost on one side where surgery had stripped the skin, and on the other tufty and uneven from the effects of repeated radiotherapy, spread about the pillow like half a greying halo. I sat across the room from her, the book I had been reading held in my lap. I said

—Do you dream, now?

She was at that stage of her illness where the weave between sleeping's warp and weft was beginning to unpick itself and I hadn't yet got used to the way that she would drift about, sliding in and out of consciousness, and when she didn't answer I thought that perhaps she had fallen asleep. Later, though, after I had put the book away and tidied the sheets, held a cup for her to drink and drawn the curtains on the fading summer night, she said

—I dream of you sometimes. Or of your father. It doesn't— she coughed

—it doesn't mean anything,

and she shifted in her bed and turned, and she was lost again.

Herbert Graf was not alone in being the subject of an analysis by his own father. Freud himself would become his daughter Anna's analyst, albeit in adulthood, and both Jung and Karl Abraham would work analytically with their children, as would Melanie Klein, an advocate of prophylactic analysis for all children, with hers; and although when I first learned about it, my fingers like a voyeur's eyes running down the indexes of college library books to find examples, it struck me as nothing but obvious intrusion on the children, incomprehensible to me in its motivation, now at least a part of that pity I felt for Herbert Graf is saved over for his father. Sometimes, when in the woods I watch my daughter with indefatigable hopefulness attempt to climb a tree whose first branch is five times her own height above the earth, tiny fingers thrust into crevasses or knots, red wellingtons scrabbling on curved bark for purchase, I feel myself winded by the desire to promise a protection that I cannot give; and if, then, I thought there was a way that I could make her life better than the ordinary – if I thought that I could make it smoother, softer, less fraught with the sudden, troubled revelation that hidden motivation brings, or with the half-rotted-through desire for what will come to haunt or hurt her – if I could give her clarity, self-knowledge, sight – and if, telling her the secret now to stop her searching for it later, I could leave happiness to her like a legacy – then I would; and if afterwards it turned out that she wasn't happy after all then how would it be possible to say it was my fault?

A month, perhaps, after Johannes and I had been to the V&A, we went to together to the Freud museum. We had met a few times during the intervening weeks, for a drink or for coffee, and one weekend we had walked together along the Thames from Cookham to Henley on a day when, after a week of better weather, winter had returned, bringing an icy, rain-flecked wind that tore at buds and stripped petals from crocuses and left us too cold and damp to be more than tolerably friendly. I thought about him often and in the evenings, in my flat with the sounds of other lives leeching through the walls, I wrote him long emails which I edited down to short emails and then didn't send; and sometimes as I turned off the lights to go to bed my phone would ring and it would be him. Our conversations were awkward. Neither of us are very good on the phone even now and it was hard then to know how we stood, me half-undressed and in the middle of a darkened flat and him elsewhere, his voice emerging in bursts from a background that might have been a party or a bar or only the noise of a busy street drifting through into my empty room.

—Well, goodnight then.

—Yes, I—

—Goodnight.

The Freud museum was my idea. Cookham had been his. I had wanted to visit the museum for years; but also I think that I wanted Johannes to believe that I was something other than I felt myself to be, a person who we both might learn to like: that person who I might have become if my mother's death and my own uncertain illness which was its aftermath had not intervened to leave my life a shoreless fluidity and myself adrift inside it. I had not visited Hampstead since the day my mother and I had lifted up the Persian carpet in my grandmother's consulting room to release a cloud of moths, but still I thought of it as in some way mine, and I assumed that recognition would be reciprocal and that it would be as I had left it, waiting. Now, though, leaving the tube at Swiss Cottage, travelling up the elderly escalator with its brass fittings and elegantly fonted signs to be spat out onto the edge of the Finchley Road, turning right towards Hampstead and leaving the churning traffic behind, I found myself wrong-footed. This was a place I hardly recognised, although it can't have been much changed. The same trees grew from the same pavements and the same houses lined them, high white stuccoed terraces with deep front steps or Edwardian mansions set back behind gardens planted with magnolia or fig, but the worlds their walls enclosed were private and I had no right of admittance to them. My grandmother and all the people that she knew were gone and I would be neither recognised nor remembered; and when, turning into Maresfield Gardens where for the last few months of his life Freud had lived in exile, cared for by his daughter, Anna, I saw in slivers eked out through windows high ceilings and broad fireplaces, bookshelves, paintings, and such gentle order, the uncrowded peace which my grandmother's flat had possessed, I felt that version of loss which is the sudden understanding of the impossibility of return, our casting out from that which memory tells us was once ours. Such an unexpected grief shook me, and by the time that Johannes arrived to find me, hands sunk deep in pockets, waiting for him in front of the museum, I had worked myself into a sullen, twitching mood I couldn't shake, my awareness that I was being unreasonable only making my sourness worse. I blamed him for my distemper. I felt that something hung between us and I resented it. I felt that perhaps I was wasting my time – here, with him – as I had wasted evenings already on unsent emails, on phone calls both imagined and real, and I wanted to take him to account but knew that in truth none of it was his fault. He, too, seemed aware that we were out of step with one another. His answers to my abruptly practical questions were brief and vague and his eyes skimmed mine, sliding off to rest elsewhere; and when, as we stood side by side to study a photograph, our hands touched, it was he who pulled himself away. In Sigmund Freud's consulting room ropes held us to a narrow tunnel in the middle of the floor and we stood, staring. The furniture here, the chairs and tables, the books and the crowded cabinets of curiosities, the couch with its drapes and cushions, had been brought over from the family's apartment in Vienna, a wholesale transportation in the spring of 1938 which had required all the resources they could call upon, both financial and administrative; and when at last they arrived these things had been unpacked and arranged to mimic the lost original so that when, after her father's death a few months later, Anna had chosen to preserve the house as it was, it was already halfway to a reliquary. I looked at it all and tried to think of my grandmother but couldn't, and so I tried to think of Anna, living and working for forty years around this preserved monument to her father's memory, a static starting point, unchallenged, unexamined, but that too slipped away from me, leaving behind Johannes – my awareness of his presence and the feeling that, somewhere in the space between us, the uncertain image of our future shivered. On the landing at the top of the beautiful staircase where a small table and a chair, overhung by a rubber plant, were set beneath a long window, I wanted to say that, one day, I would like to have such a place as this to sit; but even that felt like a presumption and so I said nothing, and neither did Johannes, and we didn't look at one another, and barely breathed; and when upstairs I found a photograph taken of one of the rooms as it had been in the late seventies, a space inhabited by Anna as an old woman, painted cabinets set against the walls and shelves of books, signifiers of an intellectual life, and between them a rather horrible armchair and, sat closely facing it, the same sort of television set that Doctor K had owned, when I remembered how towards the end of my grandmother's life the trappings of old age had intruded on her house, the television brought downstairs, electrically reclining plush armchairs placed in the rooms, and how I had felt pre-emptively bereft at the thought of what it was now too late for, the learning of that which she had been so eager to teach – the underlying, animating shape of things, the way my own cogs bit and turned – I said only

   —My grandmother had a television just like that one,

and felt such inadequacy that it almost brought me to tears.

   Descending the staircase again, I let Johannes go ahead of me into the shop and I stood for some minutes in front of a photograph of Sigmund and Anna, taken in 1913, at around the time that Freud began to see in his daughter for the first time the possibility of inheritor, no longer an often-worrying youngest daughter but a potential agent both for the perpetuation and the preservation of his work. In the photograph they walk on grass, the flat scrub of an imperfectly kept lawn, a flecked mass of unidentifiable bushes rising a few yards to their backs. Sigmund wears a hat and Anna, a step behind, her hand in the crook of his elbow, a white apron over a dirndl. Squinting slightly against the sun they have the look of people caught in a moment of unguarded intimacy, and standing staring at the picture hung just too low on the wall I felt as though I were grasping for a memory just out of reach – something to do with grass and with summer, with my grandmother in her garden and my mother, the two of them standing and thinking themselves unobserved – but for all the picture seemed significant I could make no sense of it. My memory refused to resolve into anything concrete and the photograph remained impenetrable surface, glossy, chemically rendered and preserved. I followed Johannes into the shop and found him leaning against the counter talking to the assistant, a very tall woman, younger than me, with a black polo neck and bleached hair cut into a ragged coif. She was laughing at something he had said and in the moment before he turned towards me I saw him as a stranger, and I realised that he wasn't any more, but had become in some small measure a part of my own life, a knot in that complicated tangle of utterance and experience, memory, thought, which made up my extended self.

Afterwards, after we had left the museum, we walked in silence north through Belsize Park to Hampstead Village, an aimless wander which we hoped might bring us to a pub, and as we trailed up the hill towards the heath I realised very suddenly that we were standing outside Doctor K's house. I said

—My grandmother lived here,
and Johannes, moving closer, took my hand.

During the summer of 1897 Freud conducted what he described, in a series of intensely felt letters to his friend and confidant Wilhelm Fliess, as a self-analysis. 'I believe,' he wrote, 'I am in a cocoon, and heaven knows what sort of creature will emerge from it.' Since 1891 the Freud family had been living in an apartment in Vienna, at Berggasse 19, which would remain their home until 4 June 1938 when, forced to leave at last in the wake of Austria's annexation, Freud, along with Anna and his wife Martha, would take the Orient Express to Paris and, from there, to London, first to stay in a house at the bottom of Primrose Hill and then, at last, to 20 Maresfield Gardens where, after the passing of a fine summer and the difficult completion of some remaining work, he would die at the age of eighty-three. By then his followers would regard him as a kind of secular prophet and his pronouncements, handed down through Anna, as absolute; but in 1897 he had few patients and little money, five children already and a sixth, Anna, on the way. Despite an unshakeable belief in the importance of his work he had so far failed to successfully complete a psychoanalytic treatment, and nor could he articulate any sound theory of psychoanalysis. Initially, under the influence of the neurologist Jean-Martin Charcot, with whom he had studied in Paris, he had believed that the solution to those problems of mental topology which interested him might be found in hypnosis, but he had since ceased to trust it; now he sought some alternative but seemed to get nowhere. He had been, for a while, a close collaborator with Josef Breuer but Breuer lacked Freud's faith in the idea that it was suppressed sexuality that was at the root of their patients' neurotic symptoms and, in the face of this doctrinal difference, their relationship had crumbled – a pattern which was soon to be repeated with Fliess and then, some years later, with Jung. This pattern of intense collaborative friendship followed by a difference of opinion which Freud felt as a betrayal – finding resolution at last in his relationship with Anna, whose faith in his work was absolute, a form of love, tying him to her as much as her to him – was something which Freud appeared unable either to notice or to anticipate; and I find in this a particular sadness, that a man so concerned with the possibility of understanding might remain in this case so blind. This impending separation, although still some way distant, presents itself in the letters that Freud wrote to Fliess during the summer of 1897 as a kind of weight: the oppressive, headachy closeness of the air before thunder. Freud writes with a noisy fondness, as though the volume of his friendship will keep his doubts at bay, drowning them in the performance of affection, and he allows little space for discussion of Fliess' own theories, commenting rarely on the other man's work.

The previous year Freud's father had died and, in the aftermath of loss, he found himself suffering through a period of depression. Jacob Freud had been an easy-going and rather shiftless man, cheerful but lacking any particular strength of character, his belief in the brilliance of his son certain but also lazy, a general pride often standing in for specific interest, and Freud's love for him had been tinged with the wish that he might have been a stronger and more powerful man, less biddable and easier to respect; and in the wake of his father's death Freud's awareness of this edge of near-disdain which had bounded his affection left him troubled. It was as though at the moment when Freud's father had at last passed out of life, after hovering for so long at its edge that he had begun to seem, paradoxically, invincible, Sigmund had himself been shaken, and now all the settled silt was once more muddy water. Memories, long ignored, began to surface: the sight of his mother naked in the sleeper compartment of a train when Freud was two and a half; the younger brother whose birth was the cause of jealousy until his death at the age of nine months; the adult half-brother, product of his father's first marriage, who in some barely perceptible way supplanted Sigmund in the affections of his mother; and behind all these, in shadows, the figure of his father. On 12 June he wrote to Flicss, 'I have been through some kind of a neurotic experience, with odd states of mind not intelligible to consciousness – cloudy thoughts and veiled doubts, with barely here and there a ray of light.'

Freud spent the early part of the summer travelling, first to Salzburg, where he visited his sister-in-law Minna Bernays, then to Reichenhall to see his mother, a difficult woman, dominating and egotistical, who, in contrast to his father, Freud loved uncritically. From there he returned briefly to Vienna to deal with some administrative details regarding his father's tombstone – and all the time he felt growing in himself a manifestation of those symptoms to which he was more ordinarily an observer, reliant on second-hand experience, on imperfectly communicated half-truths, so that while still trying to construct a theory of mind he must also attempt to understand the significance of omission; and all the time he must remember that his patients were also his patrons, and he must not push them. He was listless, lacking concentration. He was unable to work even when there was occasion to do so, and he had developed a tendency to disturbingly vivid dreams; but slowly, emerging from his undeniable unhappiness, came the thought that he was also being presented with an opportunity: that in himself he might find at last that willing subject whose study would bring his disordered theories into sharper focus – and so, arriving finally at the alpine resort of Aussee, where the rest of the Freud family was holidaying, he began in earnest that formal iteration of his self-analysis which would result, at last, in his theory of the unconscious. It was, at least in part, a work of mourning: an outcome of the necessary disinterment of the past that comes in the wake of loss, the going through of attics and of drawers – the process of imposing order, understanding; and, in understanding, the jettisoning of what is unimportant. To Fliess he wrote that 'the chief patient I am busy with is myself . . . This analysis is harder than any other.'

Beyond what can be inferred from his letters to Fliess, Freud left little information about the methodology of his self-analysis. That he recorded his dreams in some detail is clear from the fact that many of them, disguised in places and alongside his partially truncated interpretations, would appear as the basis of *The Interpretation of Dreams*, a work which, despite its largely unnoticed initial publication in 1899, would form the foundational text for what would become the psychoanalytic movement. In addition the struggle involved in the undertaking, which left him at times distracted and at others distraught, gave him, he claimed, a new order of sympathy for his patients—

I imagine Freud sitting all through the bright, clear summer, a middle-aged man in the mountains, grieving, the work of himself before him, and doing so I find myself fitting to the lines of him the figure of my grandmother, straight-backed at her desk each morning, hands resting on either side of her open notebook and her mind turned inwards, concentrated on those phenomena accessible only to herself. Then sympathy comes like a bloom on fruit, sudden and unlooked for, and I find that she seems softer and more human, and those morning hours no longer appear to be the execution of a grand task but only an attempt to live an ordered life. This is what we all do, after all, this striving to make sense. We bow to the drive to fit our sharp-edged pieces into a smoother shape, we clutch at agency; and perhaps my grandmother's would be the most honest way to do it, the daily effort of accounting and the acknowledgement it brings that this task can't be shirked but can only be done badly, or done well.

Despite the creative productivity of his own process of self-analysis, Freud was not convinced of its general applicability.

Analysis, he felt, required the analyst to act as a blank screen onto which the analysand's desires might be projected so that what was unconscious, unrecognised in an individual's own mind, might be made visible. To Fliess he wrote, 'True self-analysis is impossible, else there would be no illness.' Where he saw a prohibitive impossibility though I think that my grandmother saw hope: that by applying the methodology of analysis to herself she might make her own mind clear, a thing of glass in which all desire, all motivation, want, might be seen and measured. This is the promise that with effort we might be disentangled, a straight-coiled skein, and that we might find ourselves in balance; and seeing this, as I lie resting through exhausted afternoons and choke down terror at the thought that through some act of unwitting negligence my daughter might become anything other than buoyant, whole, I think that after all it is not so strange that my grandmother should have sat down each morning at the breakfast table and, like the casting of a protective spell, asked her tiny daughter to relate her dreams.

At the opposite end of the year to my visits to Hampstead, Doctor K would come and stay with us, spending Christmas in our house, ten days during which we tried to articulate our uncooperative bodies into attitudes of familial affection. From 21 December each year until the thirtieth, when she returned home to begin preparations for her New Year's Eve bridge party, Doctor K would sit at our dining room table and continue by letter those analyses which she considered to be at a crucial point, writing to her clients pages and pages of densely worded argument before returning to the routine of her own self-analysis. Her continual, unavoidable industriousness, her refusal to abandon even for such a brief time her attempts at understanding, made my mother and me uncomfortable. She filled the house with the almost-audible sound of pen on paper until we felt ourselves become periphery, ousted from our own comfort and routine, forced to deviate from those paths which habit trod for us across the carpet of the living room. My mother, ordinarily a lazy sort of cook with a tendency towards one-pot meals and the frequent provision of pasta, took refuge in the kitchen, baking parkin, peeling chestnuts, cutting tiny crosses into the bases of innumerable Brussels sprouts – food that the pair of us would eat for weeks afterwards, our mouths chewing stolidly until all reminders of our attempts to represent ourselves as something better than we were had been consumed. While my mother cooked I undertook enormously elaborate art projects, making out-of-scale nativity scenes from half-dried modelling clay and cards from paper and tinsel, or sewing as presents toys which ended up misshapen, bulbous, all these projects ill-planned and ill-executed, ill-conceived, and in the gaps necessitated by the drying of paint or glue I would make cups of tea, presenting them fresh to my mother and grandmother while the dregs of the last were still warm in the bottoms of their mugs; and in the evenings, when we sat around the gas fire eating spiced biscuits, carols on the radio, I felt myself compelled to enact a version of furious good cheer I had learned from books, a dumbshow of Christmas spirit through which my mother and grandmother might be relieved of some part of the silence of their relationship, forcing them to play games of consequences until at last, exhausted, I could go to bed.

From these winter holidays I remember with unequivocal fondness only those afternoons, Christmas Day itself and Boxing Day, when the absence of any post at all let us off the hook and we would go out into the woods behind the house and walk, bare branches like the blueprints of a church above us, black lines against the winter sky, and beneath our feet a shingle of beech nuts and the soft, crumbling litter of that year's half-rotten fall of leaves. Snow, sometimes. Frozen mud. Ice in sheets across the puddles at the bottoms of the valleys where the sun barely reached during those shortest days. Without the need to face one another we became, for the duration, three independent figures amongst the trees, released from the thrall of that complicated set of forces which inside the house defined our paths. My mother and I climbed onto fallen trees and played balancing games or searched for mushrooms, vast shelves of fungi that grew like ethereal tumours from rotten places in the wood. We told jokes, horrible old saws which made us laugh, our relief at our brief release making our voices ring. I ran ahead, testing how far into the trees I could go before sudden terror at the thought of being lost overwhelmed me; but then, circling back on ourselves and climbing the shoulder of the last ridge before home we began to quieten and still, our bodies narrowing, muscles contracting, and I felt the weight falling down on me again until we reached the front door, and, locked back into our positions, went inside.

I used to wish, during each of these Christmas holidays, that my grandmother would stop working so that we could all relax. I imagined, at the time, that this would be all it would take for our habitual selves to be returned to us, for us to meet as we did in the woods, uncompensating, not understanding then how complicated the currents are that hold us to our paths, nor how compulsive can be the tracing of them. Watching my grandmother sitting each morning at our dining table, her notebook open and expectant in front of her, I had no understanding of the drive to exhume that now turns my quiet moments into imperfect acts of reminiscence: how it is to feel that one must note each detail of one's thoughts in case that thing should pass unseen which might otherwise provide the key, laying out the shadows of the bones which rib and arch and hold the whole together. It strikes me as extraordinary, now, that we should be so hidden from ourselves, our bodies and our minds so inaccessible, in such large part uncharted; but there is a thrill to it, too: that same mixture of terror and quickening which confronts us where underneath the sea the light gives out and unnamed creatures float, eyes huge or non-existent, spines and scales unseen, or in those vast and empty tracts of space where rusting shuttles float, unmeeting. Perhaps this is what Freud felt, all through the summer of 1897, as his children played their complicated games in the shadow of the Austrian mountains and his wife, pregnant with the daughter who would become both his work and its protector, moved around him, finding things to do elsewhere – this sense of yearning outwards into darkness, the prayer for understanding that is nothing but a silent thought in a vast and vaulted space – and Röntgen, two autumns earlier, at that moment when he saw his bones laid bare: perhaps it was some version of this same desire to marvel that moved him to place his hand upon the screen, his fingers open as if waiting for an unknown gift – but the price of sight is wonder's diminishment. This was Bertha Röntgen's fear – and perhaps, after all, her refusal to look was neither stubbornness nor failure of vision but only an intuitive grasp of what a death the loss of mystery might be.

August again, the year of my father's departure, and after the first week my grandmother abandoned her attempts to get me to talk. Instead, after days during which storms of furious tears took me by surprise, embarrassing me with the evocation of a grief I wasn't aware that I felt, we would go to her consulting room, each with our allotted drink, and sit in silence, waiting out together the time until my mother might return. Doctor K did not sit straight in her chair as usual and nor did she keep her eyes on me but sat as I did, curled slightly over on herself, looking out of the window. She seemed older, that summer, than at any other time until her death. Her face was creased. She held to the same routines but seemed to do so out of habit, her mind uncharacteristically elsewhere, and during the hour each morning that she sat alone in her consulting room I would at times become aware, like waking to the drum of rain upon a roof, of the sound of her footsteps, pacing.

Anna Freud, a sixth and accidental child, was born into a bitter Viennese winter and a world in which all empty space had been already claimed. The apartment was not a small one but in addition to the five elder siblings it already contained there was Anna's nursemaid, and Sigmund and his work, and there was her mother, Martha, and Martha's sister Minna. Minna had joined the household a year earlier, taking over from Martha when she did so those tasks relating to travel and to Freud's work – the entertaining of his colleagues and the discussion of his theories, the journeys to visit the various psychoanalytic societies which had begun to coalesce in European cities – while Martha concentrated on the care of the children and the day-to-day running of the household until it came to seem at times that each of the sisters was half a wife, the presence of one allowing the other's partial retreat.

Later, it would be a favourite observation of Freud's that Anna shared a birthday with psychoanalysis, twins in whom his whole life's work was made manifest. By then she would be his Anna Antigone, her father's defence and his support, his better face, and her absolute loyalty both to himself and to his work would be rewarded by inheritance and by their names spoken in one breath, Sigmund-and-Anna, run together like a single salutation. Then, never one to miss a shot at mytholo-gising, he would think of her sometimes – young and strong and faithful when all other aspirants to his seat had proved worthless – as a Cordelia to his Lear, and his hand would creep to the beard that hid his slowly dying jaw; but at the time all that this coincidence of dates meant to either of them was that throughout Anna's early childhood Freud was absent from the second-floor flat through which the family's lives tumbled, if not physically then mentally, a fact which he would in time acknowledge, justifying his absence by remarking that such periods of inspiration will come to most of us only once in a lifetime, and even that not certain. Even when the completion of the *Interpretation of Dreams* and the end of the period of intense productivity which came in its wake left Freud with more time for his family, Anna found herself more often than not left behind, too young to accompany her father on the country walks he would take with his children or the expeditions to the boating lake. She felt herself to be overlooked and the struggle to gain that attention from her father which seemed a prerequisite for love became the defining experience of her childhood. By the time of her birth, roles had been already allotted, shared out between her brothers and her sisters so that it seemed that there was nothing left for Anna but to be pretender. It was her brother Oliver whom their father had initially marked out as his apprentice, a quick boy, bright and confident until in adolescence he began to exhibit what his father described as obsessional symptoms; to Max Eitingon, Freud would write with regret that Oliver had been 'my pride and my secret hope', failing to see the successful engineer his son had become for the analyst he wasn't. In the end, although at the urging of his father Oliver underwent analysis, it would be distance that would bring him relief: of all the Freud children it was Oliver who broke furthest from their father, leaving Vienna as 1938 washed over them not for London with the rest but for America, where the calm of this completed journey into adulthood would be shattered by the death of his only daughter, Eva, since after all the only certain thing that freedom from our parents can buy us is the right to be alone.

For Anna's own intelligence there seemed, during her early childhood, little space. It came out instead as a kind of quickness of spirit, an impish naughtiness which made her father laugh but charmed him only as a clever pet might charm, a passing diversion from more serious business. Intellect was still seen by Freud at the turn of the nineteenth century as a masculine attribute and it was not one he looked for in a daughter until all his sons, both actual and adoptive, had given him cause for disappointment; but nor did Anna feel herself physically attractive enough to aspire to a straightforward femininity. It was Anna's sister Sophie who was the pretty one, their mother's favourite and their father's pet, and her good looks seemed to bestow on her an aura too of good character of which Anna, unable to match it, was deeply envious. This envy – of Sophie's appearance and of what seemed to Anna to be her unfought-for place in their father's affections – continued throughout their childhoods until it seemed to tie them together, a falling battle that linked them more closely than any of the other Freud children. Their father watched his two unhappy daughters struggle and although it must have worried him he couldn't keep the clinician from his gaze, nor help the small hum of satisfaction as he saw played out for him those childish desires the hypothesis of which his work was based on; and if the two girls who clawed so fiercely for their father's attention sensed this and, sensing it, clung on a little harder to one another, fought a little louder, then who could blame them?

At the end of August, during the year of my father's defection, my mother came as usual to Doctor K's house to collect me but we made no preparations for departure. She arrived in the early evening and went straight to bed, and when, after I had eaten my supper in the kitchen, I was allowed upstairs to see her she looked pale and tired. I wondered if she had been crying and then the fact that I had thought of it made me feel suddenly and unwelcomely grown up. It frightened me to see her look so unhappy. It had seemed to me until that summer that the crossing into adulthood must be a transformative process, a passage through the refiner's fire during which one would be rendered down into capability, strength; but seeing my mother blinking and shell-less, her face puffy, it occurred to me for the first time that perhaps my own fears would not be shed along with the plumpness of my face but that I would always be, essentially, what I was at this moment; and not knowing what to do I started to cry myself, and stood there in the doorway weeping until my mother, taking strength from my predictable weakness, came over to me and, carrying me like a child much younger than I was, lifted me into her bed. I lay there, my tears slowed to a comfortable trickle, nestled into

112

her side until I fell asleep; but when I woke the next morning I was in my own bed again and as I went downstairs I saw that the door to my mother's room was closed. I didn't try to visit her. All day Doctor K worked and my mother stayed upstairs and – not wanting to go out, to leave the shelter of their orbits in case they ceased somehow to have the power to draw me back – I drifted through the rest of the house, trying to feel myself tentatively backwards towards a place of ignorance or balance, until at last my grandmother finished her work and came to find me.

Although usually my mother's arrival would put an end to the time that I spent in Doctor K's consulting room, that evening, by tacit agreement, we went through the heavy door and we sat opposite one another, silence holding between us like a pact we didn't expect to break, the only sounds intruding on it those of my mother moving about: the creak of the upstairs floorboards, the running of a tap, a sigh. Later still my mother came downstairs and sat for half an hour in the living room, wrapped in an old dressing gown of Doctor K's, and I curled up at her feet with my head resting on her knee. She had begun to sneeze and complained of a headache and I tried to make myself believe that her unwonted vulnerability was the result, not of any change in her or in my perception of her, but only of a summer cold that she had caught, she said, from a woman on the Northern Line who had not used a handkerchief. At dinner time Doctor K took a tray upstairs to her and I sat alone at the kitchen table, unable to summon up much appetite for my plate of scrambled eggs; and beyond the walls of the house, its undrawn curtains and blank windows, the evening faded into darkness, outside obliterated, and we three in our luminous bubble were cast adrift within the night.

On Wednesday evenings the Vienna Psychoanalytic Society met in the drawing room of the flat at Berggasse 19, and as soon as she was of an age to remain quiet Anna was allowed to sit on a small library ladder set in the corner and to listen, following as best as she was able the intense and voluble discussion of this earnest group of men who saw themselves, as the days lengthened and shortened through the early years of a new century, as architects of a future in which clarity was assured and all the convoluted crenellations of the mind would be unfolded; and there, perched in shadows, fighting sleep, Anna found an empty space in such a crowded house. It was uncomfortable balanced on the ladder's wooden top, hard to keep still, knees stiff and feet numbing from the effort to avoid drawing attention to herself, but still the narrow place she occupied gave her at last that closeness to her father which she had so desperately wanted. Sigmund, too, became within the confines of that room, for the duration of the Wednesday meetings, the father that she wanted him to be: not the easily distractible paterfamilias who gave the children rides on his back up and down the corridors of the flat or herded them through their Saturday-afternoon walks, but a man deferred to, forceful and assured, his words bearing the weight of stric-tures, a suitable object for her love.

*

August became September and the date passed that I should have returned to school, but still we remained in Doctor K's flat. It was as though we had found a way to stretch out indefinitely the moment between our injury and the onset of pain and so we stood, shock confusing us, hands clasped across the place we had been wounded, still uncertain of the damage; and I wonder now which outcome my mother dreaded most: that we should find ourselves unravelling or the opposite, that there would be no marks on us at all and, everything just as it was, the thing she had worked so hard to hold on to would slip from her grasp and become like ice in water. Each moment preceded the next in an orderly round but I had no sense of progression, and that things were not as they ought to be unsettled me, and it unsettled me more that this difference went unmentioned. That aimless procession of days which makes holidays so pleasant when carried beyond their set limits became a kind of near-intolerable, stifled tension. I had never been in Doctor K's house beyond the end of summer before and as the evenings began to smudge earlier into darkness and the air started to chill, I became increasingly aware of my displacement. In the garden leaves drifted and rosehips hardened on the bushes that the downstairs tenant had so carefully staked. On the heath, no longer crowded with picnickers, the blackberries turned. Each afternoon I stood at the kitchen window and watched as other children walked home from school, their uniforms wearing daily from sharp newness into an accustomed shell; but still inside the house we remained stuck, and could find no way to move.

*

Anna's analysis by her father, begun when she was twenty-two years old, was the culmination both of that interest in her father's work which had started during the Wednesday evenings in the Berggasse drawing room, creeping as close to her father as she dared, and of a persistent, indeterminate ill health from which she suffered throughout her adolescence. In 1907, taken to the hospital by her mother without being warned of the reason, Anna underwent an appendectomy, and although the operation itself was successful and she seemed at first to recover well she was afterwards unable to regain the weight that she had lost. She succumbed easily to colds and to chest infections and she began to be anxious, taking on a hunched, defensive posture that she struggled to overcome, and those symptoms which had at first been physical became increasingly nervous: she tended towards a periodic retreat into meticulously worked-out fantasies which would occupy her for hours, but the playing out of these narratives left her exhausted and unable to concentrate. Learning how to weave, she found in the shuttle's run a hypnotic loss of self which at first appealed but afterwards, when for whole afternoons at a time she had sat hunched over the loom until her back and fingers ached, she would reproach herself for such time lost to unawareness. Spending regular periods in sanatoria she tried to rest, enjoying fresh air and freedom from the confines of Vienna's crowds and cold weather, but felt instead cut off, apart from her family and from her father, lonely and cast out. Freud, for his part, worried that without careful management the introspective fragility that his youngest child exhibited could easily become hysteria. This sense he had of her as subject, his belief that her well-being depended on his good judgement, became another tie between them, until at last it would seem that her mind was half his own creation.

In the spring of 1913, finding himself once more bereft in the aftermath of his final break with Jung, his acute disappointment in the younger man's wilful apostasy and his grief at the loss of their friendship leading to a period of despondency which bordered on depression, Freud began for the first time to be aware of his growing practical reliance on Anna, and of the extent to which the idea of her eventual departure – into marriage, probably, since what other option might there be? – disturbed him. Sophie's recent engagement meant that soon Anna would be the only one of the children remaining at home and Freud began to feel that it was only her continued presence in the flat that staved off old age. Anna too was troubled by the implications of her own impending adulthood, feeling herself to be an uneasy fit with the world: what she would think of throughout her life as the masculine quality of her intellect sat uncomfortably with those desires she characterised as feminine – the desire for family, an interest in children. She didn't want to leave her father but as yet could not see a way of remaining with him as anything other than a dependent daughter; and although such arrangements were not unusual neither she nor Freud considered such an outcome particularly satisfactory. She spent the months approaching her eighteenth birthday and Sophie's marriage at a sanatorium in Merano, in northern Italy, troubled both by her jealousy of

117

her sister and by what she saw as her own exclusion from the preparations for the wedding, which she would in the end be judged too unwell to attend. She wrote her father fervent letters, telling him of each half pound of weight gained, each incremental advancement towards health or peace of mind; and she wrote too that 'I have read some of your books, but you should not be horrified by that, for I am already grown up and so it is no surprise that I am interested.' By the spring, although her future still felt to her both uncertain and uneasy, she had decided to start the training necessary to qualify as a teacher, successfully sitting in early summer the exam which would allow her to begin an apprenticeship in the autumn of 1914; and in the intervening weeks, by way of a rest before her training began, she travelled to England, where she hoped to develop her language skills to the point where they might be useful to her father. There she stayed with one of Freud's former patients, Loe Jones, who lived in Sussex, and together they took regular trips to London where another Jones, the unrelated Ernest, was working hard to set up and maintain an English psychoanalytic society. Ernest soon began to visit Anna, taking her on sightseeing expeditions and assuming the role of language tutor, and as a result, alerted to the relationship by Loe, Freud exercised for the first time his influence over Anna, and although he told himself that it was for her benefit, that she was both young and naïve, that she was not strong and might easily be damaged by such a relationship, he must have felt too how her marriage would have been another loss to him. To Anna he wrote, 'I have no thought of granting you the freedom of choice that your two sisters enjoyed.' For her part she said that she had never had any intention of taking the relationship further, and she felt the pull against the cord that ran between her father and herself and found for the first time both the surety of his love which she had sought since childhood and the balance of power that there is in sacrifice.

Anna returned to Vienna with the outbreak of war and began, as well as her teaching apprenticeship, a closer collaboration with her father. The continuation of the psychoanalytic movement in the face of conflict required considerable effort, with those who had been close colleagues now split by lines of allegiance. Travel between those cities where societies had sprung up became virtually impossible and mere communication only slightly less problematic. In an attempt to keep the various journals running through which the work of Freud's followers was made available, Anna spent much of her spare time in translation work, trying to ensure that language, at least, would not be a barrier to the dissemination of psychoanalytic thought. During this process Anna began to ask her father for clarification of technical terminology or of concepts that she felt herself to imperfectly understand, and out of this discussion came both the foundations for a working relationship and the first advances in what would stand between them as a kind of preliminary analysis. In the letters Anna wrote to her father when her teaching work took her away from Vienna, she began to describe to him her dreams, his own figure winding through them, as though by doing so she might tell him also something which she otherwise had no way of saying, an

119

extra burden of content to the lexicon of their emerging discipline – something about her loyalty and her love, and how, apart, she missed him: the gradual incorporation of care into their shared language.

By the time the war came to its end Anna's chronic ill health, exacerbated by four years of poor diet, made the continuation of her teaching work impossible, and so at last a decision point was reached; but facing it she found that her choice had been already made. On 1 October 1918 she entered her father's consulting room for the first time as his patient and began her teaching analysis, a culmination of those twin and twisted strands – her ill health, her interest in her father's work – which had defined her life for the best part of a decade. There were practical reasons for the choice of her father as analyst – Freud's practice had been considerably reduced by the war so that while the family as a whole had little money, particularly with the loss of Anna's teaching income, he had an unusual amount of time – but it seemed also by that point already inevitable. This was what they had been slipping towards for years, the two of them working together on their first project, which was Anna's life, their progress towards it by such slight increments that by the time Anna first knocked on her father's door it seemed only the obvious thing to do. Anna's anxious loneliness, her fixation on her father's attention, and Freud's fear that in someone else's care she might be lost to him, left no option but that the two of them turn to one another; and so six times a week for the next four years Anna opened her father's door and, stepping across the threshold, lay down upon the couch, and together they examined her until, piece by closely studied piece, they had taken her apart and built from what she had been something they could both be happy with.

In early October I sat opposite Doctor K in her consulting room and, finding in the drowsy confusion of unmarked time a sudden point of clarity, I said

—I want to go home.

Later that night, waking thirsty and going downstairs for a glass of water, I walked past the half-open door of my mother's bedroom. From around its edge light spilled, a pale wedge across the landing floorboards, and I heard the sounds of voices, my mother and my grandmother, talking softly. My grandmother said

—It would help her to talk. I could find someone.

My mother made a sound which was something like a moan, a tiny, fugitive utterance of distress, and in response to it or in defiance my grandmother said

—You could stay here. She could start school. Just for a term. She needs—

—She needs stability, that's all,

and there was silence. Moving a little I saw, framed by the doorway so that it appeared as if a picture, my grandmother sat on the edge of the bed with my mother kneeling at her feet, my mother's head bent forward and my grandmother's fingers curled into her hair; and I turned quickly, running back up the stairs, because I felt that I had intruded even by looking at an intimacy I had never known them to possess.

The next morning my mother and I packed my things into my cardboard suitcase and carried it down to sit beside my mother's bag in the front hall, my coat folded neatly on top of it. We ate lunch, all three of us, at the kitchen table, the sound of the radio filling in for conversation, and afterwards I picked up my suitcase and we said goodbye. My grandmother seemed as she always did, upright, comprehending, but as I turned at the front gate to close the latch I caught sight, for an instant, of her face as she watched us leave, and I did not understand, at the time, what her expression was, that look of long-accustomed shock, a mixture of grief and resignation, but I find myself thinking of it often, now, and wondering if it is inevitable that I, too, will in the future look that way, watching my daughter walk away from me into a complicated life that I can neither simplify nor inhabit in her stead; and I wonder what the alternative might be, and if, in fact, it might be worse.

In the end, during the last few months of my mother's life, in place of conversation or confession I read to her, picking off the shelves those same books that she had read to me in childhood, for the comfort of it and because it was a way to try and draw a link between us, so that for hours at a time we were engaged in the revisiting of worlds that we had been admitted to before, in a different configuration, when it was clearer which of the two of us led and which followed. While she drifted in and out of a sleep that grew by degrees heavier and stiller, smoothing away her features as though it were an encroaching tide that would leave, at last, nothing but clean sand where her face had been, I allowed my voice to fill the air, keeping out the silence that might otherwise have called to be filled with what I no longer had the capacity to bear. The sentences which grew from paragraphs to chapters kept us both together and apart, creating a shared space in which we could sit, each untouching of the other, but protected and encased. We were peaceful, then. The bedroom had the stillness of a pivot's turning place; and sometimes, as the evenings bled out into darkness and I found myself still reading, unable to call a halt to the day, my body's clock unwound by night wakings and the sameness of the days, I would feel as though I were becoming, in word-long increments, disconnected from the moment I inhabited, and that I was at the same time both of us, my mother and myself, stretched out across fifteen autumns, reading: the same book and the same room, the heavy curtains and the patchwork quilt, the view across the garden to where the beech trees reached across the fence. I felt, then, how easy it would be in all this placid strangeness to lose myself, and I felt how welcome it might seem to be; and when that happened I would stop reading and, putting down the book, would step quickly across the carpet and climb into my mother's bed, and I would curl up next to her, resting my head into the hollow between her shoulder and her collarbone, folding myself inwards as though by an effort of will I could contract myself back into the outlines of my five-year-old self and, doing so, regain all that I had known then: the certainty of place and order, the safety of it, the warmth. Now

123

there are nights when these positions return to me, when it is my own daughter who, climbing into bed at night for comfort, curls up beside me, and I feel my body curve into the shape my mother's did; or there are the nights of illness when I sponge my child's face, smoothing damp hair back from her forehead, and I see the outline of my mother's hands beneath the skin of mine as they go through the ritual of water and cloth, the washing-up bowl on the floor with a balled-up flannel in it, and I hear her voice in mine performing the liturgy of endearments, those sibilant invitations to returning sleep – and I wonder if these things are soothing in themselves or if it is rather that through generational repetition they have become that way, a memory taught and retaught, the epigenetics of comfort; and through these nights which ebb and flow like tides I feel memory as enactment and my mother, my grandmother, in my hands and in my arms, a half-presence, no longer quite lost.

Before my daughter was born I stood once at a wedding beside one of Johannes' cousins, watching her children run across a stretch of finely mowed grass, gentle Staffordshire hills rising in the distance against a fading sky. I had met her only a handful of times, at such large family events, and we had barely spoken beyond the exchanging of courtesies, but now, separate for some reason from the main party that continued inside, the sound of it spilling out through the mullioned windows of some repurposed country house to further emphasise our remove, we were suddenly intimate.

—It is,

she said

—like having a piece of your heart outside yourself—

meaning I suppose that a child remains a part of you, vital but detached – but this is not how it feels to me. Rather I think that it is like an amputation, something that was once joined cut off, as unrecoverable now as an object fallen from the side of a boat, drifting on the current further and further out of sight. No longer coming under the auspices of proprioception, that sourceless knowledge with which the body places its own, the lost part can now be seen, it can be weighed and measured, held, but it cannot be felt and cannot be got back. When my daughter throws her arms with thoughtless grace around my neck, I respond with an agonising gratitude that I must hide from her in case, feeling the heft of it, she might become encumbered and not do what she was born for, which is to go away from me. It is a balance – to show enough love that she is sure of me but not so much that she stays close: the fact but not the size of it – and it is an effort, as I encourage her to disentangle herself from my gaze, to discard the aching want to have her back—

Some months ago I went again to Maresfield Gardens and stood in front of the photograph of Sigmund and his daughter walking across a stretch of grass, laughing. Thinking of Anna and the forty years she spent with her father's room empty at the centre of the house, a still unconsecrated monument she had the keeping of, I wondered how often, amongst the ordinary progress of her days, the comings and goings, the journeys to the library or the shops, the letting in and out of friends, she went inside it, slipping quietly from present tense to past – and if, sitting again on the couch, leaning back against its cushions and listening to a silence which her father's voice could shape to nothing now, it was him she thought of, or herself; and after all, perhaps, instead of the sad economy of one life poured into another, what their efforts bought them was the miracle of neither having hurt the other, neither having left.

This is the crux of it: that we have no point of comparison and therefore cannot say things would have been better otherwise. I remember how it was with my daughter – how she coughed, and spat, and cried, and after being weighed was passed over to Johannes, who undid the buttons of his shirt and held her slippery, aquatic form against his freckled skin, and how from that moment on it seemed to me that the infinite stretch of possibilities she had started as began to collapse, falling away from our touch to leave behind the emergent outlines of her shape – curious, incautious, kind – and I remember how it terrified me, the suddenly yawning space between what is meant and what is done. Now that we wait to start it all again I find myself wondering if my mother felt as I do, or Doctor K, or if Max Graf did for little Hans or Freud for Anna; and, if so, how they managed to hide it – how we all do: the overwhelming fear of fucking up that having children brings, the awareness of the impossibility of not causing hurt like falling into endless water, and with it the attendant agonising understanding that what success looks like is being left behind – but what is the alternative? Only the unthinkable perfection of a preserved present. Our lives are possibility reduced to rough particularity by contact, touch, and out of it the specificity of each of us comes, so that to ask if we might have been better otherwise is to wish ourselves undone.

Interlude: Florence

It is November and I am alone in a hotel room. Outside, an unfamiliar street stretches, empty. It rains a little. We have rented a villa for a fortnight somewhere to the south of here, up in the hills – a place known to us only as a green stretch on a map and a background done in mute regret: dusty slopes planted with cypress rising behind a dozen novels of the English abroad – but we have planned badly and it is the wrong time of year, damp and chilly, mist rising instead of heat above stone terraces, a constant aching mizzle and days to fill indoors. We wanted the sort of holiday that is like a slice of time extracted from the general run of things, and with it a last pass at being just the three of us, a reminder to our daughter that completion is elastic and that she was enough even as we planned her augmentation; but we had things to finish before we could come and then there is the baby to be born when we get back, sometime during the dark and empty days stuffed deep into the gap between Christmas and New Year, so that we could neither come sooner nor wait until in the mountains there might be an outside chance of snow. We must make do with this place caught in the middle of a half-complete moult. For weeks now, oppressed at home by an ever-growing list of things that must be done before the baby comes, by clothes to be brought down from the attic and washed, nappies to be checked over, food prepared in bulk and bedding organised, bills settled, threads tied, as though at the moment of birth time will dislocate itself and these things will not be possible afterwards, I have dreamed of this room, my solitude, an empty stretch. Pregnancy has conferred on me the privileges of old age, an unquestioned pandering to my body's whims: the flight here was expected to be tiring and so Johannes has taken our daughter on ahead while I am to stay in the city resting before making the remainder of the journey tomorrow, quiet and alone on a tipped-back train seat. By the time I arrive Johannes will have organised things, mastered the geography, bought food, worked out the thermostat, and I will allow myself to be shown these things without taking the trouble to remember, my slight delay according me the status of a guest. For half of each day I will lie on a couch and the pair of them will bring me things: cups of tea, plates of biscuits, tales of their exploits. They will have adventures while I doze and I think that they have been looking forward to it, to their free immersion in those parts of themselves which exist only in my absence. Drifting in and out of sleep on the plane I heard their voices, plotting, their matched heads bent low together, and as we fell through layers of fog towards the ground they laughed.

At the airport I said goodbye to Johannes and to our daughter, and found a taxi to bring me to the hotel, and although at night, nested in pillows, I am often too uncomfortable to sleep, sat there on cracked vinyl with my legs spread to balance out the weight I do not have time to grow accustomed to, shoulders twisted, I was unconscious at once, and I stayed that way until the car reached the hotel and the driver shook me awake, tenderly in deference to my condition. Now, alone in my room, confused and chilly after the sudden rise from deep and unexpected sleep, disorientated, desolate, I sit down on the bed and start to cry. This happens to me often in pregnancy's third trimester, these sudden squalls of tears that burst from nowhere as a further reminder to me of how little my body is within my control, and there is nothing I can do but wait for it to end, this excess of emotion let out in salty water – and often it seems that waiting is all I do – for my body to complete the task it has been set, heedless of my intercession, and for the inevitable but unpredictable tract of pain beyond, for exhaustion and those first numb weeks when balance is precarious, the tumbling rush to interpret a newborn's needs. In the face of such an immediate future I find myself at a loss, those articles of rule over myself and my surroundings which I have so long taken for granted shown up as barely more substantial than a belief in prayer. I have become so accustomed to the doctrine of the mutability of pain, that suffering can be routinely eased, danger negotiated or renegotiated, that faced with its sudden failure I am terrified, as at a world remade, and I am unprepared. It seems such an unforgivable breach of promise to be reduced to flesh from which I cannot, by thought, transcend, but blood and muscle go about their business just the same and in my side something puckers, the sharp retraction of a rock pool creature that has been disturbed—

After the tears have subsided and I have had a bath that I overfilled because I am not used to my increased body mass, after I am clean again, I go out, wearing over my jeans and sweater the old waxed raincoat of Johannes' which is the only thing that does up around me now, and which forms a further layer of skin, weather-beaten and familiar, to protect me from my unexpected and abrasive loneliness. I walk with my back arched forwards and my feet splayed out, the soles of my boots slapping against the cobbles like fat flippers. I have a vague direction in mind but I am in no hurry, and I think that this gentle amble and the soft, uninterrupted patter of my thoughts against the bricks is what it is to be alone, or as alone as I can be with a head hard in my pelvis and feet against the low ridge of my ribs, kicking, and I ought to enjoy it, the respite from requirement I have so looked forward to, but instead I feel only a panicky distress, as though I had woken to find a part of myself amputated. I miss my daughter. I have become so accustomed to her shadow falling in and out of mine, to the way she forces my attention outwards, centring my awareness of space on her small form, which is at once so sturdy and so breakable, and I am used to the sound of her voice, her constant interjections drowning out the unspooling threads of my own thoughts, her commentary filling the silence where my own has gone astray. I had thought that the temporary removal of these things would be relief, that there would be no sense of loss and that I would not ache, nor feel my hands reach out to touch, to tuck back hair or pull up socks, and find my fingers land on empty air. It is not the first time I have been away. There have been days, nights; but last time she was still fat with babyhood and didn't have the power to withhold. Then she still hung from me, all mouth and fingers, and treated my presence as an unconsidered right, neither looked for nor enjoyed but only expected, so that to leave was respite, a moment when I could feel myself briefly to be whole. Now she has become something else, a mind inside a body, separate, and it seems to me that the extent of that separation from me is the extent to which I cannot bear to be apart from her. I had thought that I would continue to fall backwards into singularity as to a norm from which my deviation was temporary, and that without her I would be myself again, whole and undivided; but instead I am half-made, a house with one wall open to the wind—

and later still, returned to my hotel room, curled up under Johannes' coat like an abandoned pet, wanting the solidity of his presence, the way he stands about me like a wall, with a desire that is close to invocation, I will wonder if this is how it will always be, now, this longing to be elsewhere – the wish when I am with my daughter that I might step apart from her, and when I am apart this anxious echoing, the worry that the world might prove unsound, a counting down to her return; and I will be surprised that something so obvious has taken me so long to understand.

I get closer to the river. The dome of the cathedral rises, drizzle dulling it to the colour of London brick; behind it, hills which ought like the church's roof to awe and glorify are hidden by mist and when at last I cross the river it is nothing but water. My feet start to ache. I wonder what it says about me that I seem to feel love only in absence – that, present, I recognise only irritation, a list of inconveniences, the daily round of washing and child teas, the mundanity of looking after, and beyond this the recollection of what went before and how nice it was to be free; but I didn't recognise my freedom then – or wasn't free, since freedom only functions as an opposite to constraint. There were other things, then; and how can I say, now, that a different choice would have left me more content, and that I would not have felt the loss of this life as now I feel the loss of that one—

In the Giardino di Boboli I sit down on a bench to rest but the rain begins to fall more heavily so instead I go onwards to La Specola, where in a stone-floored room wax anatomical models lie, their hands turned upwards to show finely crafted ligaments, bones, in glass cases lined with white silk like the insides of transparent coffins. This is what I have come to see: the uncanny beauty of these delicate faces above flayed bodies, the fine tracery of silk-thread veins, the layers of flesh removable one by one to leave an empty cavity.

Aside from myself there is no one else in the room, and it is a relief to be unobserved. Standing beside the serene perfection of Clemente Susini's Anatomical Venus, half-closed eyes in a face framed by human hair and below it the open casing

134

of her thorax, her perfect lungs, her heart, and somewhere, invisible in the configuration of the museum's display, a wax-cast human child, curved and tangled and unborn. Beside her it is hard not to feel that it is I who am the imitation, mere flesh in the face of an object made, not just to educate or to instruct, but because science was once a form of worship, this stripping back of layers a way to wonder at the fierce complexity of God's work, the duty of created to creator. My own body, with its creaking joints and stretched skin, its aches and imperfections, feels by comparison to such still flesh a painful falling-short of what it ought to be. I imagine how I would look laid out like this, formed into layers, each one a shell, demountable, and at the centre of it all the indivisible nut my child makes; and how then all of it might be removed, stacked carefully up beside my open, undecaying carcass. So static I might be perfect, liable at last to a complete accounting, each piece examined, weighed and understood, disallowing surprise, mistake, decay; but amongst so much balance what would be left of me?

I return to my hotel and climb into bed, Johannes' coat on top of me, and I try to sleep so that, waking, it might be tomorrow and I might make my return to that encumbrance of minutiae, love, which anchors as much as it irks so that, tight inside its lacings, I know my shape, my place, and where my edges are.

III

Twelve weeks and four days pregnant for the first time I lay on a high metal bed, my T-shirt pulled up above the curve of my ribs and my trousers, unbuttoned, folded down to lie along my pubic bone; between them, an expanse of empty skin like tundra, unremarkable and still unrisen, a kind of fleshy middle distance. The only light in the room came from the sonographer's computer screen, its blue glow caught by her hands, the collar of her shirt, her carefully pulled-back hair. Earlier, sitting in the waiting room next to Johannes, drinking glass after glass of water and trying not to look at those who also occupied the space, the couples, the women alone, people whose lives I didn't want to give myself the right to extrapolate, the ways that they might differ from us or be the same, I had turned my face to each uniformed passer-by and anticipated in each of them a kind of jocular camaraderie, a showman's skill with patter; but the woman who had come at last to usher us through to this dim cell was so neatly professional that she seemed barely present at all, smoothed down to the perfect confines of her role. Staring at the ceiling, the exposed skin of my abdomen filling the silence like an unacknowledged solecism, I wondered if this leaching of character or compassion on her part was intentional – if it were done in case, needing either later, she might find that she had squandered them on the ordinary amongst us, we whose unborn children leaped and flipped about, indistinguishable from each other; or if it were itself an act of compassion, pre-emptive and organised: a way of sparing those for whom this day would be a shattering, insulating them from her sudden change of tone, a tightening of the skin about her mouth or eyes, the lurch from friendliness to intercession. To my left Johannes sat, bent into a plastic chair too small for him. We ought to be holding hands, I thought, but to reach him would have meant turning my arm uncomfortably backwards at the shoulder – and my reluctance to do so seemed a subtle marker of some already prevalent inadequacy in me, indelibly wrought, that I should put my own comfort first.

At last the sonographer stood up. For a minute she fiddled with the large machine beside the bed, angling its articulated monitor, then saying

—This will feel a little cold,

squeezed gel onto my stomach, a great, chilly splurt which I would afterwards be left to wipe off with a paper towel, my furtive embarrassment at the task the first in a series of slight indignities which over the next six months would strip me, layer by layer, until at last I was nothing but flesh and would lie naked in another room and scream while strangers came and went about me. The sonographer passed the ultrasound's transducer backwards and forwards, pressing down until I winced, staring across my shoulder at the monitor which Johannes and I were not yet permitted the sight of. I watched instead her face, the small frown of concentration that lay in the ridged skin between her eyes, and tried to force myself to some understanding of what we had to lose. The night before, Johannes and I had sat side by side on the sofa and, in half-made sentences like tendrils cautiously unfurling into dangerous territory, discussed what we might do, without either of us being able to quite articulate what it was we spoke about, and

—I don't know,

I said

—how I might feel. It would be dreadful—

meaning all the time that I knew what our decision would be but that I didn't know what degree of guilt or distress I might feel, all outcomes seeming to me so far entirely hypo-thetical, and I was worried I would feel nothing for this entity which was as yet more idea than child, which was in its own presumptive wellness experienced as the expectation of an unimaginably different future and as a combination of sickness and obligation, a requirement to regard my choices as circumscribed.

At last, her face relaxing into something that was almost a smile, the sonographer turned the screen around so that we could see it, her practised litany of body parts (head, legs, bladder, heart) our reward for patience. I said the things I felt

I ought to say, the exclamations of wonder or delight, and tried to make myself realise that the mass of grainy shadows on the screen was a child, and that it was ours, that it was there with us, not merely as a ghost or intimation but as something present in the room – as though the truth of it could be drummed into me by repetition.

Later, after we had paid our three pounds fifty to take home a copy of the ultrasound image that we couldn't quite bring ourselves to want and didn't know what to do with, this picture at once too intimate and too impersonal for public display, we took the bus home, the print in its cardboard sleeve tucked inside my hospital notes. The Tuesday-morning city felt strange, as when at school I would be allowed sometimes to leave at lunchtime to visit the dentist and, stepping out of the self-completeness of the classroom-bounded world, would find myself instead in one just out of whack, two degrees different from that which existed during the evenings and at weekends: a world slightly empty, industrious, quiet, its children elsewhere. Swings hung still in playgrounds. Newsagents were empty. Adults, their attention on themselves, ate sandwiches in the street. This was the same. Shadows were too sharp. There was a queue at the post office, a man sat on the steps of the library, a woman on her knees beside a crying child. The bus was half-empty but its progress was uneven, each stop a laborious rearrangement of shopping and pushchairs, and this would be my own world, soon – the buying of bananas in the afternoon, the manhandling of prams, the gratitude for open public spaces and the passing of time on benches

– a world which went about its slow business while the rest of us were elsewhere.

In the supermarket, buying bread and ham for lunch, we hovered in the dairy aisle and I asked

—Do we need milk?

and felt as though I were reading from a script. Johannes and I stood apart from one another, not touching, and although I wanted very much to be able to offer reassurance or be reassured I found that I could do neither. In the sonographer's room, both of us watching the screen, it had been as though what we looked at existed not inside my body, blood-warm, internal, but in the space between us: that what was previously a private thing, its border coextensive with myself, had been transmuted by the act of sight from subject to object. It seemed that I had, in conceiving this child, and without anticipating it, given Johannes a stake in my body; and although the extent of this was still to be negotiated, although it was a kind of temporary, partial license, like the provisional rerouting of a right of way across a private garden, still I felt this retraction of self, the shrinking back of borders to leave what had been within the perimeter now beyond the selvage. Diminished, I moved carefully, as though to protect against further incursion; but there was an obverse to it, my concession the price of purchase for my advantage. For all that it seemed to me that I had surrendered territory, still I retained the rights of ownership. The way my body interposed itself between Johannes and his child gave me an unacknowledged right to disregard him if I chose, and it gave me privilege of access, touch, an assurance of my necessary place that Johannes lacked. It was there in the way he trailed after me through hospital corridors, his presence an afterthought, and in the subtle, unarticulated presumption made by others that he would feel love less than I, or loss; but his life too had been made strange and would be altered – and so it was hard in the end to say which of us had been put more in the other's keeping. Standing in the supermarket queue behind a man buying twenty-five bottles of bathroom cleaner I saw for the first time the unintended consequences of our actions: that in choosing to have a child we had become that we had thought ourselves to be already: inextricably involved with one another, knotted up, as though a part of our child's chimerical genetics had transferred itself to us and now we were each partially the other; and so, waiting in the checkout line, we held ourselves very carefully, just apart, to save both ourselves and each other from accidental injury.

After we had eaten our sandwiches at the kitchen table, after we had returned to our separate parts of the house to work, trying to wrest from the day some semblance of the ordinary so that we might cease to feel that we were waiting, I sat at my desk. All morning, caught up in the business of appointments, I had forgotten to feel sick, but now it returned, the constant queasy ostinato over which rose exhaustion's disharmonious cadence, a progression paused before the point of resolution, aching forwards. I had no heart to work. Instead, searching for some act of petty symbolism to cast myself off from the morning, I took from a drawer of jumbled scraps a picture that I had clipped from a newspaper some months before and had not then known what to do with: the surface of Titan, the largest of Saturn's many moons, a sphere of ice and rock 5,000 kilometres in diameter swathed in a cloud of nitrogen. This image was taken by the Huygens probe, named after the Dutch astronomer who in the March of 1655, using a telescope that he had designed himself, observed Titan for the first time; 350 years later, after a journey which itself took six and a half years, the slow progress outwards into darkness of ticking metal in so much chilly silence, the probe landed with little more than thirty minutes expected battery life, this tiny span the culminating blink of so many years and such a journey. Lying on solid ground in the outer solar system, the Huygens probe then performed that minute central act it had been built for, its last process, sending back across so many slowly traversed miles this image of its resting place, an expanse of grainy ground, flattish to the horizon, with rocks or boulders strewn across it, smooth globules that might without context be taken for bubbles or for the cellular structure of a plant – and then at the picture's highest edge the sandy-coloured smoothness of the sky. I pinned the clipped-out piece of newsprint to the corkboard above my desk and next to it I put the photograph we had bought from the hospital, the ultrasound image of what would be my daughter. Looking at both of them, side by side or separately, I felt the same: a kind of plunging incomprehension, an absolute inability to make sense. These two things – a view of the ground in the outer solar system and a picture of the inside of

143

my own body, of the entity that had taken root there to build itself cell by cell towards an articulated experience of grass in sunshine or the smell of violets – existed beyond the boundaries of my constructed world, the navigable realm of named things, and into that shadowy distance which was still unmade, which had neither colour nor warmth but only spectrum and could not be spoken of except through simile (to say 'it is like this other thing' and feel the point has not been made) and I could not incorporate them: they would be neither magnified nor reduced and nor could they be imagined beyond these representations of them which were themselves little more than metaphor. Much later I saw a picture of the surface of Mars, a high-resolution image in colour, reddish-brown earth and the sharp rocks throwing shadows, and I have seen too those three-dimensional images of babies *in utero* in which each detail of their not-quite-finished faces can be picked out, their skin too smooth across the landscape of their features, their bodies foreshortened; but these did not have the same power. They were too like the images of things that are familiar: a stretch of January field, unploughed; a doll. Their strangeness has been made unrecognisable by the sharpness of their edges and although what they depict is as far from the familiar as before, they have been brought by the exactitude of these analogies within the confines of the real: I can dismiss them easily, and turn the page that they are printed on. Those two grainy pictures, though, Titan and my daughter, their figures made as if from dust or static, the ill-formed communications of ghosts, were in their strangeness absolute: they were like nothing else and so they were irresolvable and faced with them, while the child I could not imagine turned its aquatic loops in a space which I contained but couldn't reach, I could do nothing but sit, silent, and try to measure against them the implausibility of things: myself, Johannes; the particular set of events that have occurred weighed against all those that might have done, but didn't, so that our lives together seemed at times nothing but an impossibly narrow pathway rising through shadows.

On a cold winter morning in 1750 three men stood in a Covent Garden basement. In front of them, spread across a table, illuminated by that grey, early light in which facts appear immutable, lay the body of a heavily pregnant woman. Her corpse, unearthed that night from one of London's mass graveyards, had just been delivered, brought round to the back door of William Hunter's recently founded anatomy school; beyond this her history was unknown – her name and place of birth, where she had lived and how or who might mourn her, what it was that had killed her and her child so close to term that the baby's head, as they would shortly find, had already settled into her pelvis, engaging itself ready for birth. Aside from William – aspiring obstetrician and social climber, lecturer in the anatomy school which was still both novelty and controversy, with the majority of medical professionals regarding a knowledge of the body's geography as tangential to their craft – and the dead woman, whose body had become possession and exemplar, an object of interest only in its generality, in the ways that it was like all others beneath its particularising skin, those present were John Hunter, William's younger brother, and the artist Jan van Rymsdyk, who had been called quickly out of bed at the news of the woman's arrival. The body's decay, though slowed by the cold weather, necessitated haste. John had been in London barely two years and was as yet in his brother's shadow, his character and ambition not quite set, his restless curiosity still mistakable for adolescent zeal, but he had already shown himself to be a remarkable anatomist, certainly more adept than William, and so it is likely that it was he who performed the delicate operation of this unnamed woman's unpeeling: the careful parting of skin and muscle like the drawing back of heavy curtains to give sight of the horizon beyond; the injection of blood vessels with a mixture of wax and dye so that their pathways might be visible, a new-drawn map of territory claimed; and then at last the long incision in her uterus and the uncovering of that which none of them had seen before and few others had thought to look for: an unborn baby, full term, curled tightly on the pillow of its placenta. While John worked, a leather apron tied over his ordinary clothes, Jan van Rymsdyk made a series of drawings which would eventually, reproduced as engravings, form the founda-tion of William's greatest work, *The Anatomy of the Gravid Uterus Exhibited in Figures*, an atlas of the female body at each stage of pregnancy – and both John Hunter and Jan van Rymsdyk had cause to wonder, later, what fraction of the labour involved was William's that he should put his name so obviously to it. The idea, perhaps. The raising of subscriptions, later, and the hiring of engravers, true, but neither the skill of the enterprise nor its art.

These drawings, and the others that Rymsdyk would make for William Hunter over the next two decades – not all of those in the *Anatomy* were by Rymsdyk's hand but most were – are extraordinary. In these first pictures, while the woman is reduced to meaty torso, her upper body invisible or removed, the severed ends of her thigh bones visible where her legs have been sawn off, the baby is both whole and beautiful. It might be sleeping there, this child, waiting ready for the moment of that birth which has been forever put off. Its hair, where at the nape it curls, is detailed by Rymsdyk's pencil strand by strand, the neck itself a tightly folded shrug the sight of which brings back to me with an immediacy of detail the memory of my own daughter at birth, the firmness of her skin, the unexpected solidity she had like a well-packed parcel and the way she smelt, of biscuits and sweet tea. The baby's ear is flattened slightly, misshapen by long confinement as the ears of newborns often are; the fingers of its right hand curl up about its face which is hidden from us, turned in towards its mother's body as it would have done, held in her arms, in life. The other arm, stretched out, lies along the rounded body pointing up to where, beneath the lost rafters of its mother's ribs, the baby's feet lie, folded; and I can neither bear the sight of it nor turn away because in all these things I see the way that living children lie, their unconscious assumptions of protection and their trust, the way they turn towards us, sturdy bodies lying nested into half-crooked arms, and it is easy to suppose these things come into being with our sight of them and so to think ourselves responsible, deserving of credit – that it is our actions after birth that call faith forth, a child's reaction to the specificities of ourselves, our care and kindness – but the truth is that these things predate our meeting. Love exists regardless of ourselves and is unearned or got on credit, these gestures echoing those already made and made again, the child inside me turning over as I go about my business unaware, the only power that we are given to maintain or to destroy; and this is why it is such agony to hold a sleeping child: the certainty it brings us that trust is a gift, fragile like an egg in certain places, and so we must be careful with it, holding it in our outstretched hands and trying to make of them a shape that it will fit. All these things are present in Rymsdyk's drawing not as sentimentality or sympathy but only as a clear-eyed fidelity, an accuracy of line and tone: the reproduction of nothing more than what was seen.

Although it was William Hunter who claimed ownership of the work done in the Covent Garden dissecting room, it was John's life which fascinated me, his obsession with anatomy, the collection that he built throughout his life of specimens, as well as his reformation of the surgeon's craft which was effected through a kind of iron-willed iconoclasm: he had little interest in publishing his work, disdaining that which was taken on trust and considering what was written down secondary to what was seen, but only set about his business in the way he thought it should be done until at last the world began to follow him. Looking at the pictures from *Anatomy of the*

Gravid Uterus now, though, it is neither John nor William that I think of but the artist, Jan van Rymsdyk, standing with his chalk box at John's shoulder, his fingers stiffened by the cold, trying to keep the edges of his paper clean while in the corner of the room the discarded parts of already rotting human bodies lay in piles. Beyond his work as a medical illustrator little of the detail of Rymsdyk's life remains. He was born in the Netherlands but the place and the year are lost, as is the date of his arrival in England or what he did on reaching it, where he lived in London, or the manner of his life between the winter mornings hunched in the dissecting room. It is possible that William Hunter gave him lodging in order that he would be readily available when his skills were needed, time being critical to the examination of the body's fine structures, its vessels and membranes that start to deteriorate as soon as death occurs; certainly John would go on to make such arrangements with other artists. What is clear is that Rymsdyk was not happy with the kind of work that he was doing. He had ambitions: a portrait artist, perhaps. A recorder of the living. Anything beyond these chilly rooms, this stink. In 1758, eight years after he made his first drawing for William Hunter, Rymsdyk left London for Bristol, where he was determined to set himself up as portraitist; but he was not a success. He took lodgings for himself and his young son, Andrew, whose mother is another blank face at the periphery of the remembered or recorded, and he placed advertisements, trying to position himself as far as possible from his surgical labours, but little work came, and what did retained a tinge of

149

the mortuary: he painted the portrait of the surgeon William Barrett who had hoped, perhaps, by paying for this service to access Rymsdyk's greater talent; but on that score he was refused. Failing to find work he considered acceptable Rymsdyk was reduced to painting inn signs, funding by that means a moderate drunkenness and a life that was considered squalid even in such squalid times, relying for the rest on Barrett's petty charities – occasional meals, the passing on of cast-off clothes – until at last, in 1764, he accepted defeat and returned to London. There, resentful, he went back to the work that he had left behind, beginning again after such an ignoble hiatus on illustrations for William Hunter's *Gravid Uterus* and working in addition with John, who, himself recently returned to London from a stint as an army surgeon in Portugal and trying now to build his own reputation aside from his brother, had entered into partnership with a dentist and was spending his spare time trying to graft human teeth onto the heads of cockerels. Rymsdyk continued this work for another six years, but something must have altered in him on his return to London from Bristol – some sting, perhaps, of humiliation which he turned to determination – because he did not return to the impecuniousness of his West Country life but saved his money until he had enough to begin on what he had begun to think of as his own great work: in 1772 he applied to the British Museum for permission, with his son Andrew, to draw their exhibits, making from them an encyclopaedia of his own, *Museum Britannicum*, which was published at last in 1778. In the preface he allows himself finally to vent a lifetime's frustration, the resentments of a man who feels his skills to be unrecognised, uncredited, taken advantage of, who considered William Hunter to have manipulated him, persuading him out of a respectable career in order that he should continue to prostitute his skills on corpses – but thinking of Rymsdyk it is this image that comes most clearly to me: the reflection of a dissection-room window, its cold clear light, striations around it as in rippled water, caught on the membrane stretched across a five-month-old foetus' bent head, the uterine home of this almost-child removed and placed upon a wooden table; and this drawn, just as it was seen, by a man whose talent lay precisely in this – the reproduction of the surface of things. This is the mean tragedy I imagine for Jan van Rymsdyk: not that of skill wasted nor diverted so much as a skill half-made, an artist incapable of artifice. Seeing, he was capable only of reproduction, eye to hand: the surface of things stretched across his paper, each fold of skin, each hair, the shadow on a cheek, a fingernail, an eyelid closed. In his drawings of William Hunter's specimens this is enough, or it is already too much – the viewer can do the rest, the very fact of the subject's existence exciting pathos; but given a living subject, one less arousing of compassionate terror, I imagine Rymsdyk's work as unresounding, the dull thud of a language spoken without understanding. His subjects would be, on canvas, no more than themselves, and perhaps not even that: Rymsdyk could add no character, could inflect his subject with neither meaning nor significance beyond that which they manifested themselves. The world, for him, was nothing but what was, his talent in its reproduction; and from his intimation of this lack, his awareness of something missing without any conception of what it was, his bitterness rose.

Finding out that I was pregnant after months of disappointment tinged with unnameable relief, I sat down and cried and couldn't say why. Johannes sat next to me, uncertain but not unsympathetic. Expecting to feel joy or at least an end to the anxiety of small plastic strips in silent bathrooms and the hurriedly suppressed disappointment on Johannes' face I felt instead something that was closer to grief: a kind of fracture, the past lost and the future suddenly made opaque, certainty of habit or routine removed. It was not a surprise but still it felt a shock, and all evening I stayed where I was, curled up beneath a blanket on the sofa leaking tears while Johannes sat next to me, worried and quiet. I clung to him and tried to remember that I was not alone without yet understanding the full import of it: that aloneness now was in the past, and that I might come to long for it, the stillness of a body unkicked, from inside or out.

The next morning I rang the doctor's surgery but

—Can you tell me the reason for your appointment?

found myself unable to say the words. It seemed still too much of a presumption to place myself among the ranks of the pregnant with their unlearned competencies, their experiences that I lacked. Later, sitting in the surgery listening to the doctor's well-rehearsed speech, which was delivered to the empty space above my left ear while one of his hands fiddled with his computer mouse, the dancing cursor wishing me gone, I waited for the moment that he would call me out and demand proof, but it seemed that my honesty was assumed – and after all why would I lie. He said

—Take paracetamol for your headaches.

—I don't get headaches any more.

—You might now. How are you feeling otherwise?

—A little tired—

although really I had no idea how I felt and nor did I have any gauge against which I could measure what was normal. There would be mornings, soon, when I would lie on the bathroom floor, too tired to move except when another swell of nausea came and forced me up over the toilet bowl to retch emptily; and still, then, I wouldn't know whether this was within the parameters of the ordinary and anyway what could be done about it but endure. The doctor shrugged a little and turned away.

—If you have any pain or bleeding go to A & E,

and so began the slow dividing up of time: two thirds of a year split into months, and months split into weeks and days, each one counted off as though it were a sentence to be passed and at the end of it recalibration, a return to an old life with new circumstances like a house that has been gutted and rebuilt. Walking out of the doctor's surgery, my place within the system confirmed, my status acknowledged, clutching a sheaf of leaflets on birth options, hospital choices, the risks associated with shellfish, coffee, cheese, I looked at other women sideways, wondering. I sat on the bus and felt myself

153

to be an imposter in both worlds: no longer singular but not yet past the point at which I could consider myself to be what other pregnant women were – and even after birth, that ten-hour lesson in topography during which I heard myself call out but couldn't understand the words, I felt that I had not quite done things properly and that my own experience lacked, in some way, that element necessary to transform it into knowledge: that it remained not the thing itself but only a picture of it, so that I was not quite yet a mother. Placental failure and my own rising blood pressure had forced us to tip our daughter early outwards and, lacking the benefit of properly delivered nutrition and those last few consolidating weeks, she was at birth a half-size model of herself, her blueish skin stretched tight across her skull, the line of her vertebrae showing along her back like threaded pearls beneath a cotton sheet. She lay near weightless in my arms, her eyelids falling across her steady gaze, and I was almost afraid to touch her. Home from the hospital, crying again, I had to ask Johannes to pick her up and put her down, to change her clothes, to hand her to me to feed because I was too frightened of the feel of her; and so we began to count again, not down this time but up, back through days and weeks to months, and still that joy I had been promised didn't come. I waited, patiently, through all the dark extended hours for the instant of my own remaking when at last I would feel the things I ought: certainty, transparency, delight; but it didn't come. Instead there was only something complicated that I didn't have a name for, quite – a shifting landscape of duty and fear, the gnawing, restless anxiety that started when I was in a different room from my daughter and the exhausted relief when she was calm and slept; the growing realisation that I would always now be pulled in two directions and that I would be filled with the compulsion to protect, which meant that even when I felt I couldn't bear another minute of it I pulled myself up in bed and reached out in darkness for the crying child; and it baffles me now that I couldn't see how all this added up to love. I can't remember quite when it was that shock subsided and I came at last to understand that what I had taken for a temporary loss of balance was only how things always would be, this tangle of broken sleep and piles of washing left on chairs the sum total of motherhood's difference so that I must come to terms, and find a way to live in tiny interludes – except that it had, I think, something to do with routine: this new life laid down in daily patterns, a structure ossified by repetition until I could barely remember what it had been like before and so could not compare; and even then I could not say for certain that I was happy but only that the thought of things being otherwise was unbearable—

but all this was to come. For those first few weeks of pregnancy, as slowly sickness became coextensive with consciousness, and exhaustion accrued mass until it was so solid that I could make no dent in it, I felt, in place of the anticipated joy, only a tiny, private sense of loss, and, beyond that – as I went about the necessary administration, the choosing of a hospital, the midwife's booking-in appointment, as I provided urine samples and had my blood drawn into vials – an overarching disbelief that despite all evidence to the contrary I would, at the end of it, have a child.

On 21 December 1767, seventeen years after he had performed the dissection of a pregnant woman while his brother William watched and the artist Jan van Rymsdyk sketched, John Hunter again stood beside a woman's body, this one alive, albeit not for much longer, and with a name: Martha Rhodes. She was twenty-three years old, less than five feet tall and with a pelvis that was contorted to such a degree it was making the delivery of the child that she was carrying impossible. She had gone into labour the day before and the midwife, unable to provide any relief, had called for Henry Thomson, a surgeon at the London Hospital; he in turn had called for John Hunter to assist him in attempting to perform a Caesarean section. Although of the three who had been present at the Covent Garden dissection it was William who had become the obstetrician, still it was John who had the reputation for skill and for experiment; besides which, William had ascended smoothly to that strata of society he had always looked to join and was now physician to Queen Charlotte – he would not come here, to this house in Rose and Crown Court off Shoe Lane, one of those narrow alleys that lead upwards from Fleet Street, away from the river. There were others present, too, besides Henry Thompson and John: a gaggle of men, physicians and surgeons, gathered like jostling birds around the table on which Martha lay, her head resting on a pillow and her legs hanging down. None of them had performed this operation before and nor had they seen it done.

156

It was curiosity which brought them up the twisting staircase, the anticipation of something extraordinary done before them, and I imagine that there would have been amongst them a carnival atmosphere, an excitement close to joy, hands shaken firmly to greet each new arrival, shoulders clasped, as two and a half centuries later another group would gather to wait for the results of the Huygens probe, those first pictures of a strange moon, or as the crowds on the Boulevard des Capucines would wait in line all afternoon, wrapped up against the cold, to watch an infant Andrée Lumiere pat the surface of a goldfish bowl: this expectation of a line pushed back and something beyond it grasped, knowledge delivered into light and them as witnesses. Martha's terror I cannot imagine. Thomson said she consented to the operation 'cheerfully' but it seems hard to believe. Perhaps he mistook exhaustion for fortitude, the desperation to have suffering ended by any means for equanimity at the prospect of the route proposed – and I remember how, late on in labour when it seemed that everything had been this way for as long as I could remember and that there would never be an end to it, unknown people came and went about me, obstetricians, midwives, anaesthetists, and I grabbed at any hand that I could reach and begged. Martha must have known for months how things would be; hoped, perhaps, that the baby would be small so that they both might have the ordinary chances, death a risk but not a certainty, this portion of hope making the whole seem possible; and I wonder if she lay awake through long, uncomfortable nights while the baby kicked against her tangled vertebrae weighing her child's life against her own, her mind ticking through all possible outcomes until, her body having shown no sign of offering reprieve, all that was left to her was this table, these men, the dose of opium that they gave her. There are times when pregnancy seems like the narrowing down of options to a point, and still it is impossible to make oneself believe, quite, that there is no way out of it but this: a bed somewhere, a costing up of risks and this pain that tears you from yourself, your mind disbursed by it, your body made an exit wound. Even now, when what I wait for is a path that has been mapped, its route no longer trod in darkness but seen and softened, when there are epidurals, ultrasound, the surgeon's manifold experience, my body imaged, patterned, known – even now I am terrified.

Thomson made the cut in Martha's belly. He reached in with his unwashed hands and pulled out the child, who cried; with the baby gone Martha's uterus began to contract with a suddenness that took the men by surprise so that John Hunter had to help by holding in the mass of intestines which spilled out into the resulting space. Thomson stitched the wound shut and when the needle pierced Martha's skin she cried out, and this was, Thomson said, the only sign of anguish that she gave. She died five hours later; the baby survived her by two days. Neither Thomson nor Hunter were present at her death although they attended to her again afterwards, for her autopsy, to which William Hunter also came. They could not find any immediate cause for her death, but in the notes that he appended to Thomson's account of the operation John Hunter wrote that 'an author would be more esteemed and relied

158

upon, if, with candour and disinterestedness, he would relate the instances wherein he has failed, that the world might judge how far the chance or hazard of the operation rendered it advisable or not' – and progress is incremental, slow, and it is cruel, but it is made. In 1793 one of John Hunter's pupils will assist at a Caesarean after which the woman will survive.

The night after the scan I lay with my belly pressed against Johannes' back, listening to his slow breathing, each round ending with a snore, my long-worn irritation at the sound a form of habitual affection. Earlier in the evening, intending to put a pile of laundry away, I had come up to our bedroom and, suddenly overwhelmed, had lain down across the bed and pulled a blanket over me and fallen asleep. Johannes had woken me when he came up, helping me to pull off my clothes, shaking out the duvet where the weight of my body had flattened it; and now, although still heavy with tiredness, disorientated and chilly, sleep would not return. I shut my eyes and felt in imagination along the plane where the two of us did not quite join, our impenetrable skins closely separating, giving warmth but withholding access, each touch an affirmation both of proximity and disjunction, and I thought of the baby, that thing which lay between us, still more mine than his. The child was, for Johannes, still largely hypothetical: his life so far remained predominantly unchanged and what I felt as a set of prohibitions and a physical incapacity, a slow-fast-slow remaking of my own biology, was for him hardly more than anticipation, like waiting for Christmas to come – the gradual, enjoyable winding-up of affairs before the holidays. He would not feel the child's weight until he held it in his arms, an object, loved but as apart as he and I were: a thing to be learned, understood from the outside as a puzzle or a book is understood, imperfectly, wholeheartedly. Things were not, for him, so ambiguous: the harbouring of a stranger inside oneself, this the closest to another person it is possible to be but that person still unnamed, unmet. I had tried, while walking sometimes through the city in the afternoons, to reach inwards and find some connection to my unborn child, but I was not one of those who felt able to talk to it, to feel intimacy, and for me the sense of being unwell, of being incapacitated, remained immediate while my child was a distant thing, floating in a space that was a kind of void to which I had no access. This is what John Hunter found, that chilly morning in the basement of his brother's Covent Garden house as he bent over the flayed, dismembered body of a woman: that even inside the womb, intimacy is incomplete. Injecting with deft fingers the fine capillaries of the placenta, more gentle in his dealings with this already decomposing tissue than he would ever have been while it was still alive, he found two separate systems: the infant's and the mother's, coextensive but not conjoined, so that they were like the maps of two mazes interleaved, path laid on path but uncrossable, each leading back only into itself. My child and I shared breath, and we shared water, food, but we remained distinct: the line between us was a cell's breadth across but still it held us back from falling into one another and we were not the same.

Lying by Johannes in the darkness, envying him the unquestioned habit of sleep, the way he could remove himself, I wished that I might pause, take stock; and this is a thought that comes to me again now: that I would like to pause pregnancy like a film, to walk away, do something else, returning later when I have had time to rest or think. I would like to be unpregnant for a stretch. I had always, before my first pregnancy, regarded my body as a kind of tool, a necessary mechanism, largely self-sustaining, which, unless malfunctioning, did what I instructed of it, and so to have my agency so abruptly curtailed, revealed as little more than conceit, felt like a betrayal. I no longer listened to my own command. Inside me, while I wished that I might be able to be elsewhere, that I might leave my body in the frowsty sheets and go downstairs to sit in the dark kitchen, unswollen and cool, cells split to cells, thoughtless and ascending, forming heart and lungs, eyes, ears – a hand grew nails – this child already going about its business, its still uncomprehending mind unreachable, apart.

If Jan van Rymsdyk's talent was to see only the surface of things then John Hunter's commensurate gift, perhaps, was to see how this surface might be extended: the folds in it, the crenellations that could be laid flat. Where for others the human body had seemed a single entity, one impassive mechanism, feared more than it was understood, to Hunter it was an urn and his task its excavation, gone about in winter when the weather held its rotting back: the disinterment of our long-hidden contents, the heavy organs, lungs, lymphatic system, the tree-like patterns veins make, the chambers of the heart. Seeing them, weighing them in his hands, feeling their give beneath the blade of his knife or watching pigmented wax bring ersatz life to a cadaver's bloodless tissue, he hoped to gain something – not quite fame but something close to it, renown or vindication, and with it the satisfaction of his curiosity. Since the dark ages when plague came in waves to wash whole villages clean of their inhabitants, European medicine had been largely a matter of propitiation, being more akin to faith than science: a set of habitual, heritable practices based on the untested superstition that any intervention has a better chance of success than nothing at all. What conception of the healthy function of the human body existed was based on the humour system developed by the ancient Greeks, the acknowledgement of its insusceptibility to any kind of contemporary proof buried beneath the lingering belief that humanity was in decline and what had once been obvious was now mysterious, absorbable only by rote. Treatment was a combination of quackery, alchemy, and religion, its methods unchanged for generations, passed down from master to apprentice in a training system which required neither a knowledge of anatomy nor any practical skill beyond the performing of those techniques which were considered to constitute medicine and were demanded as much by the patient as they were prescribed by the physician: bloodletting, cupping, prayer, the occasional hacking off of parts. Where elsewhere the Enlightenment had begun to prise things open at the joints, medicine lagged

162

behind, staid – susceptible to doctrine rather than proof, debate rather than experiment; and into this miasma John Hunter's curiosity fell like a sharp illumination.

His interest in anatomy, both human and animal, began in childhood. He was born during the second week of February 1728 at Long Calderwood, his family's farm which stood in the countryside south of Glasgow. The actual date of his birth is a matter of dispute: although he himself always celebrated it on the fourteenth it was recorded in the parish register as the thirteenth and in the family Bible as the seventh. He was the youngest of ten, and perhaps after so many the arrival of another child was routine, or, three of them having died already before he was born, perhaps his mother had learned that birth was no guarantee of life and so did not – yet – allow herself to give too much away, the lurch of affection that is betrayed by announcement, and this was why his birthday was forgotten; or perhaps it was only that he came swiftly into a world where there was work to be done, the ewes lambing out on the hillsides being more immediately important to a family with no other source of income and now another child to feed and clothe. As a boy he possessed neither an interest in nor an aptitude for schoolwork. He found reading a laborious task and one to be avoided, its rewards pale compared to those which could be got from an examination of the world outside the schoolroom, and often on his morning walk along the lane to the kirk for lessons he would allow himself to become diverted, curiosity leading him to spend long hours when he ought to have been at his books roaming about the countryside instead. His early life became a journey of investigation through leaf mould, through the mud along the sides of streams or underneath the hedges; and during these empty, meandering childhood days John began to learn by experiment the art of dissection, poking about in the remains of dead sheep he found on the hillsides or eviscerating earthworms, skinning mice and shrews. In adulthood this dislike of academic study became a principle of sorts – he distrusted that which might be learned from books, believing that it was always better to see for oneself with truth not proved until it had been performed.

John's adolescence was marked by loss. When he was thirteen his father died, swiftly followed by two of his sisters. Shortly after he turned seventeen his eldest brother, James, whose progress through his chosen medical career had taken him to London, became unable to work due to ill health and returned to the farm, lying for days on one of the beds that pulled out from the walls of the two-roomed cottage like drawers, coughing himself to death at last while John watched or was nearby; and I find it hard to imagine, now, when death is largely hedged about with treatment plans, when it does not often come senseless out of nowhere but can be postponed, or if not that then at least explained, what grief must have been like when that boundary was a curtain you could put your hand through. It is easy to think that when death could be so quickly turned to, a matter of misstep, and all families counted lost children in their numbers, that loss must have been a blunter thing – that, having so much practice, they must have been better at it, or inoculated, that it cannot have been for them such devastation, this laying waste – as the birth of a tenth child might be of less account in a busy week than the loss of a pair of lambs, so that the date of it was not looked for until later, when it was found to have been forgotten. It is easy to think that in an age without anaesthetics, when legs might be hacked off on kitchen tables, teeth pulled with pliers taking gobbets of jaw and gum away with them, that pain must have been somehow a less precise, less devastating thing, the alternative being unthinkable – that it was just the same but, persisting, could only be endured, too universal to allow concession; and so John Hunter watched the bodies of those he loved carried out of the tiny farmhouse one by one, making their last journey to the church, and afterwards he went about the business of his days, he went to school or to the fields, and then at last, summoned by William, the sole surviving brother he barely remembered, he went to London, and did not return.

Sometimes, walking down the street or looking outwards from the window of a bus, I saw a child run to take its mother's hand or, stretching itself upwards, be swung into a father's arms, their faces turned to one another, intimate, engrossed, and then I felt a swift pain like an upwards stab, my anticipation of this future I was in the process of laying down. Across those strangers' faces I saw our own elided, mine and Johannes', the child's who was half-turned away; but although in the other two I saw imagination's present of perfection it was my own that I bent towards, trying to trace in its lines the better version of myself I still waited to succumb to, someone steady, solid, rooted down – and this was the first intimation I had of the complicated interplay between our children and ourselves, the ways we twine about one another, using them as mirrors to our flaws, their reflective plasticity showing us how we must first learn that which we would like to teach: honesty, patience, the capacity to put another first. It seemed, at times, an act of profound selfishness, to have a child so that I might become a parent; but selfish, too, to have a child and stay the same, or not to have one – unless the only honest choice would have been to try to become this kinder version of myself without the need to bring another into it. Once my daughter was born, of course, so much was simplified: I could not now regret any aspect of her, or wish her unmade, or do anything but try to turn myself into the thing she needed, but still I wonder sometimes if I was right to foist life, and myself, upon her; if I am right to do it again because I want her to have an ally and cannot bear the thought of never holding another sleeping baby, the agony of their eyelids, their mouths, their skin. Perhaps it is an unjustifiable act – no reason for it quite good, quite generous enough. To feel myself tired of a life which stretched out like fine sand without much weather, to be dissatisfied, wanting to become the shape a child would force me into, must stand as sufficient explanation, an ill-formulated defence; and thinking this, sat on the bus's upper deck, my forehead resting on the window's sweating glass, I would hold my hands, momentarily, across my stomach, and feel it for what it was, for me: a kind of promise I must strive to keep, the

166

commitment to make myself the best mother I could to make up for having made myself one at all.

I would like to say of John Hunter's adolescent losses that they must have been formative, bringing about through their repetition the long inculcation of a desire to save, as I would like to see in my daughter's birth a wheel rotating: the transmutation of the lives of others, lost, into a capacity for something else – kindness or happiness or an incrementally increasing volume of compassion; but I can't make myself believe it. Such events are not crucibles but are only the natural order of things, what happens and then what happens after it – the same striations of grief and its easing that all of us suffer, to some degree. Looking back, we might try to make sense – to stand in a calm spot, latterly, and examine at leisure the details of a running tumble we barely kept pace with, the cumulative outcome of decisions made blindly or not at all, and try and find significance in it, some repetition of a universal pattern played out in ourselves. This would be comfort: to believe both that things could not have been other than they were and that how they were was right, one's life a well-formed argument, each moment a logical progression from the last.

In the afternoons, home from Italy and waiting out the shortening late-autumn days, I sit upstairs while Johannes and our daughter play outside, running through the drifts of fallen leaves that skirt the garden or lifting up stones to see what lives beneath them, and I watch them through the window and feel how precarious things are. All this will soon be lost. The solstice will be passed, and Christmas, and the new baby will be born, buds will come on the trees again and our daughter's tiny figure which seems at every moment so complete will be superseded by another version of itself. I would like to believe that what we have made of our lives is good or at least that it is inevitable, and so I try to find in all that has happened a pattern or a thread, some shape beyond the turn of past to future. I search for meaning everywhere. It is as if I believe that I might, drawing back a swathe of cloth left in an attic, find comprehension waiting for me, and with it a final understanding of the way things are, and why, and that in doing so I might feel the fragility of things less; but there is nothing there. Meaning is not found, discovered in a cold basement with an artist lurking, or as an image unexpectedly projected on a screen, but is assigned, the task of its superimposition upon what exists no more than an inelegant scramble to keep up; and underneath it nothing but events come willy-nilly into being and our need to fill the days, decisions leading to decisions, a mapless ramble, haunting and unthought-through.

The journey from Long Calderwood to Covent Garden, made in the late September of 1748, took John Hunter two weeks, at the end of which he presented himself at his brother's house, a rough young man, travel-worn, grubby, given to casual obscenity and with a stubborn refusal to temper his manners that he would maintain throughout his life, the first sign of that uncompromising streak which would manifest later as an absolute commitment to progress in the face of a largely intractable establishment. He would work as his brother's assistant for twelve years, quickly becoming the more skilled of the two in matters of dissection so that soon he was performing almost all of the anatomical work of the school, both the routine preparation of cadavers for demonstration and the more specialised work necessary to the preservation of body parts for permanent display. At last his health began to give out, the result of overwork or of those long hours spent amongst the rot and filth of the dissection room – it would be another century before Lister introduced the idea of hand-washing to surgery and John's fingernails would have been crusted under with remnants of the tissues, living and dead, that he had been working on; or perhaps he wanted only an excuse to extricate himself from William's benevolent indenture. Lacking, despite his experience, any of those formal qualifications which would allow him to set up as a surgeon in private practice, but wanting access to the same proliferation of live subjects as he had already observed dead, he joined the army, a course of action which would have the added benefit of circumventing the need for qualification, since an army surgeon, demobbed, had an automatic right to practice on the general population; and in March 1761 he set sail on board a hospital ship to take part in the assault by the British on Belle-Île, an island off the coast of Brittany.

Battlefield medicine was a desperate affair. In an initial failed attempt upon the island, John found himself stepping across the bodies of the wounded where they had been thrown upon the decks, waiting for their limbs to be sawn through, for lead shot or wooden splinters to be excised from the flesh of chests or flanks, the slashed skin flayed half off the heads of men to be stitched shut as best as could be managed. Deaths must have occurred from a multitude of causes: the wounds themselves and attendant blood loss but also from shock resultant upon the brutality of treatment or from infections introduced while the wounds were being enlarged, standard practice to allow foreign bodies to be removed more easily. In such conditions, men's flesh cut away without sanitation or disinfection on board a ship or in the churned mud beside a battlefield, any procedure was liable to be rendered worse than useless, and infection was so ubiquitous that suppuration was considered by surgeons of the time to be a necessary part of healing. John Hunter, watching his colleagues going about their business with the surety of those who doubt neither their purpose nor their methodology, while around them men screamed, and bled, and died, began to wonder what the point was of practices which seemed to him to save no one. Later, after April and reinforcements brought a second and successful assault upon the island, John would come across five French soldiers, wounded by gunfire, who had taken refuge in an empty farmhouse. Their wounds – despite no medical attention – had healed as well, if not better, than those who had experienced all the supposed benefits of the ministration of a surgeon. John began to modify his practice accordingly, treating only those injuries where treatment seemed an absolute necessity. He advocated too that surgery should be delayed if possible until the patient was no longer lying on the battlefield but was somewhere relatively comfortable, and until their condition had to some degree stabilised, particularly in the case of amputations – and although despite these adaptations of standard practice many men still died it was not quite so many, which John Hunter, despite the opposition and at times derision of his colleagues, considered proof.

On a wet Saturday morning, Johannes and I went to see his mother to tell her that I was pregnant. She picked us up from the station in her car as she always did and drove us back to the tall and narrow house Johannes had grown up in, him in the front talking about the general progress of his work and me, trying not to be sick, in the back. The house, cleaned for our arrival, felt unoccupied, as though it were up to us to claim the space, leaving our jumpers on the backs of chairs as marks of ownership, our socks balled up in corners, our books spine-upwards on the sofa cushions, the dust motes floating in the light from the hallway window gusted by the currents that our voices and our moving bodies made. We carried our things up to the bedroom in which we would sleep and while Johannes went back down I unpacked my pyjamas and the bag with our toothbrushes and toothpaste in it, then set to untangling the coiled wire of my phone charger, stringing these tasks out for as long as I could. I hoped that Johannes might tell his mother while I was up there so that I might be spared, because I have always hated the breaking of news, the imparting of information which will affect another's life in however slight a way. I find it horrible to think that others might have such power over me, always: that at any moment there might be someone in a room elsewhere planning the best way to break open my life. Earlier I had asked Johannes, hearing myself sound petulant

—Can't you call her first and tell her so it won't be a surprise?

but Johannes, frowning, said

—She'll prefer it this way,

and so I waited for as long as I could before going downstairs to where Johannes and his mother sat at the well-scrubbed kitchen table, the old green teapot and a silence like elastic set between them. I went to stand by Johannes' shoulder as though he might shield me and he held my hand as at last he spoke; and afterwards in the relief of having got it over with I felt a little giddy, prone to confidences, and we drank our tea and made plans and the gentle chatter of the radio turned on in the corner lent our conversation a pleasing intimacy, as though we were afraid, in this otherwise empty house, of being overheard.

Later I lay resting in the neat spare room while Johannes sat downstairs reading or watching television. There was a knock on the door and his mother came in, bringing me up a glass of warm milk with honey in it and some ginger biscuits from a batch that she had made earlier that afternoon, her hands deep in a jar of flour while I sat in a chair and watched her, wondering if such easy competence, such orderly familiarity with the making of things, was a skill that I might ever achieve. She placed the plate of biscuits and the milk on the bedside table and when I asked her she fetched me a glass of water as well because I was always thirsty. This gentle solicitude felt at that moment like a slight return to childhood, like being put to bed with flu and having the doctor come, that certainty of being protected, and as she moved about me, arranging things, I realised that this was what I had been longing for: to have someone place themselves between me and adulthood, taking away for a while the necessity to make sense of things. She sat down on the bed beside me and took my hand.

—How are you feeling?

she asked and

—Okay,

I said,

—Tired.

I told her that there were days when I went to bed straight after dinner, the evening news not yet finished on the radio, and although I slept all night when I woke in the morning still I felt the same exhaustion, a chemical thing, utterly undentable. I asked

—Is this how everyone feels?

and she told me how when pregnant with Johannes, working in a theatre, she would go during every break she had to lie down in the room in the costume department where the washing machines were kept and, lulled by their constant grumbling and the rocking of their spin cycles, she would sleep. Then, she said, after Johannes was born, for weeks the only place he would reliably sleep was in front of the washing machine, and so she would set his Moses basket down on the floor in their galley kitchen and put a load of washing on and he would sleep for the whole cycle; and not wanting to leave him alone, this her first child and his fragility unquantifiable, she would pull a duvet down from the bedroom upstairs and wrap herself in it and she would lie on the floor next to him and she would sleep, too, both of them calmed by the rattle of the spinning drum.

—In the first few weeks after a new baby is born you do things like that,

she said, telling me that it was a slight and temporary madness brought on by exhaustion – the trauma of a birth you don't have time to recover from and the need to find any pattern amongst so much endless chaos, any routine, however tenuous, and any continuity of preference which might allow you to feel that you know this tiny stranger who has ripped so much apart: your body, your home, your life. I thought of these words often in the days after my daughter was born when I suffered from an acute but transitory agoraphobia, a terror that if I took the baby outside I would become incapable, unable to protect her from some catastrophe I could neither imagine nor name. Each day I forced myself to put her in a sling, her body nestled tight against me, so that I might walk to the end of the road and back while Johannes stood at the front door and watched me as I asked him to, his expression one of kindness without understanding, and I held the thought of Johannes' mother like a talisman – this tall and capable woman, determined, calm, lying with her baby for hours each day on the kitchen floor, manufacturing washing just for the peace – and it comforted me. Now, sat in her spare room discussing in low voices the trivia of our own experiences, I felt for the first time between the two of us the taut lines of a relationship that was not triangulated through Johannes: being each a part of this child's life we were now tied to one another and this tie was indissoluble – could be evaded, perhaps, but neither destroyed nor forgotten. This new intimacy was an unintended consequence but I recognised it too as something that I longed for, a surer place in this house, a claim over this woman's care; and I wondered if it was partly why I had been chary of coming here, because I could see how it might be an imposition, effected without her consent and not subject to her protest.

After she had gone I lay in bed, peaceful for the first time in weeks, and thought of my own mother, how what I had been feeling the lack of since the evening that I found out that I was pregnant was not the particularity of her, but rather the role she might have occupied and the fulfilment of those tasks for whose performance she would have been the obvious candidate; and this is what I miss still, now: a sense of enduring belonging, the knowledge that a place is mine regardless of the extent to which I might merit it. I would have that undemanded, undemanding love, not dependent on individuals but rather on the places that they hold – mother, daughter; except that as I no longer hold that place I cannot now imagine how it might feel to do so, since to cease to have a mother is to forget, as well, how to be a daughter. Lying in the bed at Johannes' mother's house, I could neither transpose myself backwards nor see my own mother alive, our relationship forged into adulthood. What space she might have occupied had long ago been filled or had silted up – and this is the thing about death, that time lessens hurt but multiplies loss. I wanted to be able to say that after all it would have been better to have my own mother there than Johannes' but I couldn't, because the thought of it was an empty hypothesis; and because while my own mother had faded into imperfect memory Johannes' was here, present, a woman whose feet creaked across the floorboards of the room next door – and since I found I didn't want my mother there I found that I also missed her terribly.

Leaving the army after three years, John Hunter began the long struggle to establish himself in his profession. He worked at first as a dentist, pursuing an interest in the transplantation of human teeth, pulling them from the heads of those who needed the money and placing them instead in the mouths of those who could afford to pay. These rudimentary transplants would, he noticed, have greater success if the donor tooth was fresh, and if it was approximately the same size as that which had been lost, and although none of his transplants would have been fully successful some of them are reported to have remained in place for a period of years, which was a considerable achievement for the time. In 1764 he set up his own anatomy school, a rival establishment to William's, and he began, at last, in private practice, on top of which he pursued his own research, working late and rising early and experimenting with little in the way of ethical concern on both his patients and, almost certainly, on himself. Money was always an issue.

In addition to the ever-expanding London premises needed to house both his family and pupils, and his growing collection of surgical preparations, as soon as he could afford to he took a country house at Earl's Court where he kept a menagerie, a collection of animals of greater or lesser exoticism which he observed in life and then, dead, took to pieces. He took the temperature of hibernating hedgehogs, fed dye to pigs to prove that bone growth occurs by accumulation at the outer ends, collected fossils, crossbred dogs with jackals. To Edward Jenner, friend and ex-pupil, he wrote, 'I have but one order to send you which is send every thing you can get either animal vegetable or mineral, and the compound of the two viz either animal or vegetable mineralised.'

Jenner, who after three years as John's pupil had turned down an offer of a partnership, had left London in 1773 to return to his native Gloucestershire and a country practice; but the two maintained their relationship by correspondence, Jenner's letters lost but John's surviving, ungrammatical, enthused, a list of requests to be sent hedgehogs and cuckoos, eels, porpoise, along with instructions for experiments to be performed, treatments to be tried. The specimens sent by Jenner and those gleaned from Hunter's Earl's Court zoo along with thousands of others – skeletons hung from wires, soft tissues pickled in jars and skins dried, venous networks transcribed in wax – form Hunter's greatest monument: a vast collection, a testament to skill and curiosity which he nearly bankrupted himself to maintain and which was saved, after his death, by the dedicated ministrations of his last apprentice,

William Clift, to become at last the museum of the Royal College of Surgeons, housed now in their premises behind Holborn station. Walking through it one Saturday afternoon with Johannes, nearing the end of my first pregnancy, I felt at that vast catalogue of the interior, the mechanics of living things, an awe that bordered on bafflement, something important written too large for me to comprehend. Setting out from home we had intended to visit the John Soane museum, that other extraordinary monument to the eighteenth-century collectors' art which sits on the opposite side of Lincoln's Inn Fields from the Hunterian, its contents a map of that which is neither skin nor muscle but which seems, in the narrow corridors of Soane's house, to be as traceable. We had been there several times before and, planning with Johannes a last afternoon spent in that casual, wandering pursuit of curiosity which had made up so much of our leisure time to date but which would soon become, we supposed, less possible, I had thought immediately of the John Soane, its dim rooms and cluttered walls, its jokes, the monk's cell and the sarcophagus and the tiny gallery with its paintings fixed to shutters so that a man with a sort of boat hook has to open them for you one by one to reveal the vast and complicated skies of Turner, the satirical figures of Hogarth's modern moral subjects. It is a place that has always given me, stepping over the threshold, a rush of delight, the joy that something so extraordinary should exist; but arriving that day with Johannes we found the museum closed for a private event and so made our way instead around the dusty perimeter of Lincoln's Inn Fields, its central stretch of grass browned by the summer's heat to straw, past the tall red-brick gate leading to the inn itself, to the Royal College of Surgeons on the first floor of which, in a double-height gallery of glass cases, the Hunterian museum is housed.

—Are you sure,

Johannes had said that morning as I struggled to tie my own shoelaces

—you wouldn't rather stay at home?

but I had been determined. It had always seemed to me during the long, meandering weekend days which had formed such a large part of our lives to date as though, while we were looking at these artefacts of other lives, something important was not quite being said, an utterance that existed in the spaces between our words and tied us, in our silent understanding of it, together; and we had taken it for granted, this intimate harmonic which implied concordance, until it was gone. All week, through another appointment with the midwife, the doctor, through a discussion of birth plans and a consideration of the relative merits of muslin brands, Moses baskets, this proliferation of necessary trivia which had come upon me like a curse, I had felt myself becoming increasingly unfamiliar, emptied out of all the thoughts I'd had before and refilled with these new concerns; and the stranger I became the stranger too Johannes was, different and far away, until the old presumption of case was replaced with an algorithm of concern and debt. When we were alone together, when we sat down to eat or when we walked in the park during the long, light evenings, our pace a poor equivocation between Johannes' long stride and my ponderous shamble, I was not peaceful but spoke at length, planning out a future that we hadn't yet the means to imagine, my speech an obsessive examination of the possible ways that we might live after the baby was born, how we might divide the labour up, and what we needed, what there was to do and what might be left till later. I harangued and argued with myself, considered out loud the possible effects of a weight of historical wrongs, the flaws in our respective characters, the way I wished things might be done, as though I might talk myself into quietness or as though, by talking, I might call into being there between the heavy summer alders the best possible version of ourselves – as though I might make myself ready; but I could not prepare myself for something so unknown nor find any way across the next months except by living them, and so my monologue was little more than benediction, the filling up of empty space with prayer. I didn't know what to do with myself otherwise. All that I had been before I had given up already and the emptiness was appalling. I twitched to be active and longed to feel Johannes close again and so I insisted that we fill our time with those things we had always done and then, embarked upon them, was angered by my inability to see them through, or exhausted by my stubborn perseverance. Through all this Johannes was patient, or he seemed that way to me; but even his patience was unsatisfactory. I wanted something more than calm capitulation to my ill-made plans, attention to my tumbled words. I wanted him to care as much as I did about those things which I wished I could not care about myself, or I wanted him to tell me how dull I had become so that in retaliation I might break myself open against him, crack violently through this shell that separated us, and we might be ourselves again—

As we walked through the gift shop and into the museum I said

—We could go for lunch after this. We could go to the Seven Stars. Or to somewhere on the South Bank. We could have dim sum.

—Won't you be tired?

Johannes asked, and because I was already tired, because I wished that I was at home and that we had never come out, because my feet ached and the baby kicking was a constant irritation, I pulled my hand away from his and let him go on ahead.

At a meeting of the Royal Society on 27 January 1780, thirty years after William had watched and Rymsdyk had sketched while John teased apart the fabric of a nameless woman's uterus, twenty-six years after William published under his own name the discovery of the mechanism of placental blood supply, John accused William of plagiarism. This was, perhaps, the result of a long-festering complaint: that for all the work John had done for William during the twelve years he had been his assistant, John had received no credit, and nor had he been able to take ownership of any of the preparations that he had made during that time and which now formed the nexus of William's own collection, leaving John's, though its specimens were now numbered in the thousands, always incomplete. Being unable to rectify this wrong, he niggled at that which would have seemed to him the lesser – the apportioning of published credit – although in the end there would be no satisfactory outcome to this dispute for either party. The Royal Society would refuse to publish John's paper. William, beyond a single confused and confusing response, would offer no defence but, on his death, would leave every part of his fortune including the farmhouse at Long Calderwood to his nephew Matthew Baillie, and his collection to the University of Glasgow; and, subsequently, it would turn out that priority for the discovery would after all go to neither brother but to a Dutch anatomist, Wilhelm Noortwyk, who had demonstrated the separation of maternal and foetal blood supply in 1743.

Standing in the museum, surrounded by the relics of John Hunter's quest for understanding, his attempts to enumerate what a person is, how we are made, our solid, ordinary parts assembled into something greater, a whole which can be neither contained nor comprehended – I watched Johannes walk from case to case, past the fish, the fossils, the cockerel's head with a human tooth rising from its comb like a jaunty hat, and I felt familiarity drift from him like dust until he too was nothing but parts, unidentifiable amongst so many. He paused by the skeleton of Charles Byrne, the Irish giant whose body Hunter kept against his wishes, stealing the corpse from its lead coffin as it was transported by cart to the Kent coast for burial at sea, and I saw the hunch of Johannes' shoulders, the slight tip of his head which indicated silent disapproval, and although I knew these things as well as the feeling of my own breath rising in my lungs, for a moment I recognised him not as the complicated, sprawling pattern memory makes from faces, the words uttered and unuttered, the promises preserved, revoked, this mess of accord and arguments – that intangible nexus of thought, our own and others', which makes us who we are – but only as mechanism. There is nothing more horrible than this: a world elucidated and all that is seen, understood. Johannes turned and, catching my look, came back to where I stood and said

—Shall we go home?

and

—Yes,

I answered, and felt better at last, having found my way to this defeat.

Then there are these other moments, the ones it is so easy to forget: an evening, unremarkable. Light pooling on the ceiling from the lamps, the curtains closed. I surface from a doze to find Johannes sat beside me on the bed, reading, and half-turning towards him I reach out my hand; he takes it without looking, his fingers as they always are, dry and warm, their familiarity like the kinder obverse to desire. We do not speak but, less apart, we settle back into ourselves. I close my eyes – this moment comes again and then again, our children sleeping or unborn: the mute reiteration of the certainty that all is well, and we are as we ought to be.

*

John Hunter died on 16 October 1793 and it is hard, at times, to find quite what it was that he left us, beyond the macabre and serried rows of jars that made up his collection. So many of his experiments, taken all in all, were failures – the transplanted teeth, the Caesarean, the operations after which his patients, lacking the advantages of antiseptics, died. Perhaps, after all, it was only this: the understanding that we are objects and that we might be learned – that there is no mystery, but that we might look and see ourselves. Three years after his death, Edward Jenner, who had been his first pupil and lifelong friend, would inoculate an eight-year-old boy against smallpox. This boy would be one of twenty-three subjects on whom Jenner performed the experiment; subsequently he exposed the boy to smallpox and found that he was immune; and this was Jenner's contribution: not that he should have used cowpox as a vaccine – a practice which had been standard in Britain since the 1720s but in use elsewhere for centuries – but that he should have proved that it worked. To him, in one of the first of the letters between them, Hunter had written, 'But why do you ask me a question, by the way of solving it. I think your solution is just; but why think, why not trie the Expt.'

This another moment of clarity: sent to hospital by a midwife because, with the Doppler receiver set against the smooth dome of my rising abdomen, something hadn't sounded right. I lay on the sofa with my clothes disarranged while she went about the business of folding her things away, putting on her coat, and I tried to gauge from her movements how urgent this was.

—Do I need to go right now?

I asked, and she replied

—You might as well,

so I stood up and found a jumper, socks, and called out to Johannes, who asked

—Should I come with you?

but though I wanted him to, and though I wanted him to know it without it being said, still it seemed absurd to drag him to sit for hours in a hospital when he might be at home and comfortable. I said

—I'll be okay,

and so he contented himself with packing a bag for me, filling a bottle with water, finding my keys; and then as I put on my shoes he stood in the middle of the room, his own feet bare against the floorboards, this tiny detail of our difference prompting me to go to him and put my arms around him, to comfort him, because while in this sudden situation, which was not yet an emergency but which might turn out, later on, looking backwards, to be the start of one, we were both incapable of altering the outcome, I at least was necessary while he, no less concerned, was left behind.

Later, behind a curtain, I sat next to a foetal heartbeat monitor, its sensors attached to me by long belts whose buckles were held in place with ratty knots. A midwife had spent some time adjusting them and now I was able to move only slightly, an arm or leg shifted by millimetres, in case they slipped and the monitor could no longer get a reading. Every now and then the baby moved, turning this way or that, so that the machine could no longer detect a heartbeat and an alarm went off, and then I would sit there, waiting, listening to its dull beeping until the midwife came back again to readjust the straps. Next to me, across an unspooling sheet of paper, a thin line traced the pattern of the baby's heart, its peaks and troughs a litany of all that was – and although at first I could think only how uncomfortable I was, how afraid, after a while it seemed that watching this line, the steady pace it kept, its spitting progress up and down, something which had long occluded fell away at last and certainty was left behind. This was fear's gift, perhaps, this sharpened vision, and in the transcription of my own child's fragile heart I could read at last not quite love, not connection nor communion, but rather the understanding that what was important was only the way we stood to one another, protected and protector, and that we had gone beyond argument and must get on with things.

A few weeks ago, looking in the bottom of a drawer for something else, I found a photo of my mother – saved, somehow, when so much else has been thrown away. In it, she is standing in front of a wall up which sunflowers grow, their circular faces higher than her head. She wears a short-sleeved Fair Isle jumper, a denim skirt, bare legs. She looks very young, and in her arms she holds her newborn child. I have pinned the picture up above my desk, between the two foetal scans and the newspaper clipping of Saturn's moon, and, looking at it, I find that when I think of my mother now it is not of that version of herself which she became when ill, nor of how she was when, throughout my childhood, compromise forced her into unspectacular unhappiness, but rather it is of this woman whom I never knew, whose face bends down to meet her child's, whose hands enclose, who smiles. I feel such tenderness towards her. She must have known so little, then, of what it is to have a child, but had to learn it all from scratch, and did – as I have done, and all the rest of us, learning from the moment we are born how to be one single version of ourselves with all the losses that entails. I am so used to thinking of my mother as someone who is complete, her life concluded, that to imagine her at this moment, caught during those few weeks when everything was, briefly and for both of us, possibility, is to feel her startlingly close, her death unwound. She is not shut and done with but persists, and I am glad.

In the end there was nothing obviously wrong with the baby except that one of the midwives, her hand pressing hard into the flesh of my belly, suspected she was breech. A scan confirmed it, the baby's feet crossed over in my pelvis, her head tucked in beneath my ribs, turned to one side with her hands held up in front of her face, their fingers flexing, as though she were examining their tiny nails for dirt. I was sent to the waiting room until a doctor had time to see me; and it seems to me now, looking back, that from this point onwards pregnancy became for me a series of waits on uncomfortable chairs, so that very soon I became accustomed to it, to the boredom and the occasional startling kindnesses, to the opening hours of the cafe in the hospital foyer and the smell in the corridors, the doors which opened and shut and the women behind them, crying on their knees, these just-caught glimpses of female agony, and to the way they looked afterwards, this cohort of which I was not yet a part, to their exhausted faces lit up with surprise above their freshly minted children as though at the sudden comprehension of a lesson it had taken them nine months to learn; but this first time it was new. I sat very upright and wished that Johannes was there. After a while I asked the receptionist if there would be time for me to go to the cafe and get something to eat; she said she didn't know but would see what she could do. Ten more minutes passed and she brought me an egg sandwich which was fridge cold and tasted strongly of margarine but I was grateful for it anyway and felt better afterwards. At last the doctor came and called me and, stiffly, I followed him into a tiny office. He told me his name and I forgot it instantly. I sat down. He shuffled some pieces of paper and said

—Baby's breech, I see.

I felt a kind of anxious shame, as though it were a dereliction of duty that had brought me here, my own failure to marshal my flesh and control my unborn child. I was afraid that, seeing inside me, he would find the means to judge what I hadn't even known existed and couldn't recognise although I too had seen it on the screen, that pattern of dark and light which the inside of my own body made.

—We can book you in for an ECV and try to turn the baby manually. It's a bit uncomfortable and there is a small risk of—

I tried hard to focus on what was being said but my mind wandered. I already knew that I would do what this man told me and there was a comfort in the acceptance of my surrender. It seemed that what was being talked of was not my body but only an object in the space between us, predictable and mundane, and of which he, having more experience, was the better judge – all I did was carry it about.

—These leaflets will explain—

My grandmother and I had sat like this, facing one another. It was, I thought, the same time of day, although this doctor and I were deep inside the hospital and there was no window, no sound but the footsteps of the nurses and the bleeping of machines, and in place of sweating glasses there were two plastic cups from the water fountain in the corner of the waiting room. I held mine in my hands.

—You will need to sign—

My grandmother too had tried this: to make me explicit to myself in order that I might better be able to decide how to act; and although hers was another kind of explanation it held the same promise: the resolution of a complicated pattern into one that could be understood, her voice that of the radiologist – there are the feet, the hands, there is the head. Here is want, desire, and here is fear, here anger, love. At times my grandmother's promise of transparency has seemed to me like a gift and at others like an act of violence; but always it has seemed to me that something important was left out of it, the understanding which she searched for missed, lost in that gap between an object and its name. Even

189

so I felt the power of it and do so still: how simple things would be if only I could know myself or others; if, stepping in between a light source and a screen, I could see the way that I was constituted, those hidden structures, the bones, the joints that give the rest its shape – and then I might know something for certain, that I was alive or that I would be dead, these two differently slanted articulations of the same fundamental understanding; but instead there is only this excavation, a digging in the dark: precarious, uncertain, impossible to complete.

All these same anxieties I feel again now. I am worried about the distance between Johannes and myself, between us both and our daughter. I am worried that the particular circumstances pregnancy forces on us will not retreat with its ending. I am worried that I will fail to be an adequate mother; that I will neither recognise nor love my child. I am worried that I have failed already, somehow; that failure has been written into my genetics or my history and will be passed on, crossing over that fragile barrier the placenta makes to infect this unknown person for whom I ought to be a shield. I am afraid of all that which, unseen, remains unknown: my own insides, the thoughts of others, the future. This baby has turned already, head downwards, waiting to be born. My daughter draws pictures of it, the three of us with our feet on a flat green line of ground and the baby floating in the air. Sometimes it is tethered to me or to Johannes by a drawn-on string and at others it only drifts, there in the empty space above us. Johannes' mother is coming for Christmas. She will stay until after the baby is born.

I lay on another bed in another room while a consultant obstetrician pushed my unborn daughter round through the skin of my stomach, forcing her to turn by 180 degrees. I tried not to scream with the pain of it. Afterwards I sat for another hour attached to the monitor; the baby was fine but, someone else said, seemed rather small. They would do another scan. I lost track, then, of whom the people were who came and went about me, of the appointments attended, the waiting rooms inhabited. It ceased to seem important. My blood pressure was taken often; it rose a little and then came down again but each rise took it higher than the last. I was warned about vision changes, headaches, swelling of the hands or feet. At home I lay on the sofa and read or slept. Johannes tried to work. Late each afternoon we walked around the park, our steps slow, and stopped afterwards at a pub where Johannes drank cider and I a pint of lime and soda, the cordial making viscous swirls inside the glass. We said very little. It seemed that without our noticing it, without anything having been said or done, intimacy had returned, and we stood together, waiting, for what was both our end and our beginning. I had bought a Moses basket, several packs of Babygros, a swaddling blanket; there was nothing left to do. I no longer felt the need to talk. We went to Johannes' mother's for the weekend and I read detective novels in the garden. I couldn't sleep at night but no longer felt tired, only rather empty: an end might come at any moment but while inevitable it remained out of reach, since how is it ever possible to imagine in advance how one might get from there to here. There were more scans, more machines; the baby was still small but no one seemed to know what it meant, and it seemed at times that we might stay this way forever, autumn never coming, nor the baby; and then at thirty-seven weeks I sat again in a doctor's office. Johannes was at home, his own life a thread less frayed than mine, his hours contiguous while mine drifted apart.

—Your blood pressure is very high.

I told the doctor that hospitals always made me anxious and she smiled. There was another scan, so many now that I had stopped trying to see the screen. She said

—I need to speak to the consultant,

and while she was gone I sat alone in the room and thought of nothing at all. When she came back she looked brisk, her face betraying anxiety with a slightly too-stiff brightness, and I remembered the sonographer, and how she had seemed to disappear behind efficiency.

—We'd like you to come back tomorrow to be induced.

I don't know what I had expected but it wasn't this: a bag packed ready in the hall and a bus ride to the hospital in the morning, two days spent walking round and round the hospital car park in the hope that labour might begin and then a doctor breaking my waters with a kind of pin; an oxytocin drip; the feeling that my body was turning itself inside out. I remember it only in snatches: a radio playing in the corner and Johannes' hand on my forehead, the gas which made me feel dizzy and the throwing up of half a tuna sandwich into a paper bowl, and how I lay and begged, calling out for something to be done—

then this, the moment all else falls away from. The pain stops and someone hands my daughter to me, her tiny body beating at the air, and for an instant we are nothing but a single surface, joined, laid out beneath the light, and everything is perfect, clear: I know her absolutely and all her history is mine for I have seen it all—

then time, then growth obscures. The cord is cut; our separation starts. She is taken from me, weighed, dressed. I close my eyes in relief that it is over and a first part of her life is lost to me. Johannes holds her. She starts to cry, a newborn's wail of bleak surprise, and we do not know the reason but must try, somehow, to find it out.

Acknowledgements

That this book was written at all is due in large part to the support, encouragement and deadlines I received from both my agent, Jack Ramm, and my editor at John Murray, Mark Richards. All good bits should be considered to their credit. Bad bits are mine alone.

Thanks are also due to Ed Lake, for a certain amount of drink and conversation, and to Lyn Curthoys, whose fortnightly journeys along the Metropolitan Line gave me time.

Finally, thank you as always to Ben, who has never questioned the importance of my work to me, but who has built us a life into which it fits.

Further Reading

The following is a list of works which were particularly useful in the writing of this book. Much of my reading was done at the Wellcome Library. It is a wonderful place, and I recommend it to everyone.

Part I

Bleich, Alan Ralph, *The Story of X-rays: From Rontgen to Isotopes*, Dover Publications, 1960

Glasser, Otto, *Wilhelm Conrad Rontgen and the Early History of the Rontgen Rays*, Norman Publishing, 1989

Kevles, Bettyann, *Naked to the Bone: Medical Imaging in the Twentieth Century*, Rutgers University Press, 1997

Rontgen, Wilhelm Conrad, 'On a New Kind of Rays' (trans. Arthur Stanton from the Sitzungsberichte der Würzburger Physik-medic Gesellschaft, 1895), *Nature*, 23 January 1896

Part II

Anzieu, Didier, *Freud's Self Analysis* (trans. Peter Graham), Hogarth Press, 1986

Freud, Sigmund (ed. Marie Bonaparte, Anna Freud, Ernst Kris), *The Origins of Psycho-Analysis: Letters to Wilhelm Fliess, Drafts and Notes, 1887–1902* (trans. Eric Mosbacher and James Strachey), Imago, 1954

Freud, Sigmund, *Case Histories, Dora and Little Hans*, Pelican, 1977

Gay, Peter, *Freud: A Life for Our Time*, Anchor Books, 1989

Symington, Neville, *The Analytic Experience: Lectures from the Tavistock*, Free Association Books, 1986

Young-Bruehl, Elisabeth, *Anna Freud*, Macmillan, 1989

Interlude

Ebenstein, Joanna, *The Anatomical Venus*, Thames & Hudson, 2016

Part III

'An Account of the Performing of the Caesarean Operation, with remarks, by Mr Henry Thomson, Surgeon to the London Hospital, Communicated by Dr Hunter', *Medical Observations and Inquiries*, 4, 1779

Hunter, John, *Letters from the Past: From John Hunter to Edward Jenner*, Royal College of Surgeons of England, 1976

Moore, Wendy, *The Knife Man: Blood, Body Snatching, and the Birth of Modern Surgery*, Bantam, 2005

Thornton, John Leonard, *Jan Van Rymsdyk: Medical Illustrator of the Eighteenth Century*, Oleander Press, 1981

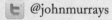
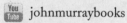
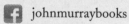